Cody Hawks
& the Chosen One

Cody Hawks

AND THE
CHOSEN ONE

Book 0.5

Visit Mandi Oyster online at
www.MandiOyster.com

Facebook: https://www.facebook.com/MandiOysterAuthor
Instagram: https://www.instagram.com/MandiOyster/

*This book is dedicated to all of the indie authors
out there working a full-time job while writing.*

We can do this!

Chapter 1

New Beginning

Cody raced over the roads faster than he should. His Camaro sat low to the ground, hugging the curves of the mountain road. Britny, his only sister, was sick, so his parents had grudgingly decided to stay behind with her.

A part of Cody wanted them with him for the transition into this new stage of his life, but the other part knew they wouldn't approve of the speed he was driving. If it weren't for Dacia, he would slow down, but the nightmare he'd had last night wouldn't stop playing through his mind.

Shadows chased after Dacia, tendrils of darkness swirled around her, reaching for her, grabbing at her arms and legs, trying to pull her back. Her red hair bounced against her shoulders as she sprinted away from them. Fear widened her emerald eyes. Her breathing was harsh.

Whatever this was, she wouldn't be able to outrun it, and if it came for Dacia, Cody would be there for her. He would *always* be there for her.

The dreams had started the summer before second grade. They always featured a red-headed girl. At first, Cody hadn't understood why he was having the nightmares, but on the first day of school, the teacher had stood in front of the class with a little girl hiding behind her legs. The teacher stepped back, and the girl cowered. Her eyes were ringed in dark circles, and she looked haunted.

Cody had recognized her immediately. His heart pounded a little faster as he forced himself to stay in his seat. He'd wanted to jump up and stand in front of her, to protect her from the stares of the other kids. Instead, he'd clutched his desk while he watched her.

Her hands had been clasped together in front of her, and she'd twisted her fingers back and forth. She stared down at the black-flecked white tiles, never lifting her gaze.

"Class, this is Dacia Wolf," Mrs. Winters had said, oblivious to the girl's discomfort.

Daysha. The name echoed through Cody's head. He'd never heard it before.

"Her family just moved to Bittersweet." The teacher had bent down, moving her face a little closer to the girl, causing her to flinch. "Can you tell us something about yourself?"

Dacia's curls swung around her, hitting her cheeks as she shook her head.

"No, not even where you moved from or what brought you here?" Mrs. Winters had rested her hand on Dacia's shoulder in what appeared to be a comforting gesture, but the girl had cringed.

Tears had leaked out of her eyes, trailing down her face and dripping off of her chin, but she hadn't wiped them away. Watching her, he'd wondered if she hoped nobody would notice. Then he'd realized that he noticed everything about her. He'd never paid much attention to girls before. Everybody knew they were weird … but not her.

This girl he wouldn't ignore. She needed him. He couldn't explain how he'd known it, but she did.

Mrs. Winters had pursed her lips before looking around the room. "Okay, then. Why don't you take a seat over there between Cody and Sidney?"

Cody had watched the whole thing, wondering how this girl that he'd dreamt about for months suddenly stood in front of him. He'd watched her night after night. Sometimes, she would outrun the monsters and the darkness. Other times, she had died.

From the first moment he'd seen her, Cody had felt drawn to her. He'd wanted to protect her from whatever made her look so haunted.

He'd never told Dacia about the nightmares. Until last night, he'd thought they were gone. This time, something felt different about it, though. There had been an urgency to his nightmare that made him wish he'd come with her yesterday.

He hated that she was alone. She didn't warm up to people easily. It had taken him months to gain her trust, and as far as he knew, he was still the only person that she'd truly opened up to.

Fear tightened his stomach, and he pressed his foot down on the gas pedal even harder. He needed to get to her and make sure she was okay.

He slowed down when he passed the stone sign that welcomed him to Phlox University. The road curved again, giving him an uninterrupted view of The Snowfire Mountains. Falcon Lake was nestled below the towering slopes, but he was too distracted to appreciate the beauty surrounding him.

He turned into the parking lot that separated the men's and women's dorms and peeled his hands off the steering wheel, flexing and unflexing them several times to get the blood pumping into his fingertips. Then he rolled his neck, trying to loosen some of the tension he'd picked up on the three-hour drive. He looked at the clock on his radio. Maybe he'd wait an hour or so to let his parents know he'd made it.

Grabbing his Bittersweet Lions hoodie off the seat, he opened the door and got out. Dacia was jogging across the parking lot toward him. He pulled his sweatshirt over his head, stuffed his hands into the pockets of his blue jeans, and leaned against his car, watching her.

The wind caught her hair, blowing it around her face. The image was so like his dream that his knees buckled. If it wouldn't have been for her smile, he would have run to her to protect her from whatever it was that hunted her.

Even from this far away, he admired the sparkle in her eyes. Freckles splattered her nose and rosy cheeks. She was beautiful, even more so because she didn't know it or spend hours trying to be.

He couldn't stop the grin from spreading over his face as she neared him. Somehow, she didn't know how he felt about her, and he would do anything to keep it that way. He couldn't jeopardize their friendship. She needed him, and he would never risk that.

"Hey, where are your parents?" She stopped and looked around the parking lot, most likely expecting to see their SUV.

He tried to act nonchalant but knew she would see through him anyway. "Britny's not feeling good, so I told them to stay and take care of her."

She ran her hand from his shoulder to just below his elbow, then left it there. He could feel the warmth of her fingers through his hoodie. Thousands of butterflies took flight in his stomach, and his heart raced. He needed to lighten the mood, or she'd figure it out, but he couldn't force himself to move or to look away from her. He stared at her too long.

"What?" Her voice trembled just slightly. "Do I have something on my face?"

"Besides the freckles?" He laughed, hoping the intensity of his gaze hadn't been too much, and clutched his hand inside his pocket. The desire to touch her face was worse than he'd ever experienced. He'd spent too long worrying about her. "No"—he hoped his voice didn't sound as husky as he thought it did—"your eyes are really green today."

Crimson rushed up from her neck, coating her face and ears, and she twirled a curl around her finger. He wasn't making things any easier on himself. He'd always found her insecurities endearing.

"Help me carry my stuff?" He turned away from her before he said or did something he would regret. She'd never given him any indication that she wanted to be more than friends, and he wouldn't pressure her.

Chapter 2
Burning Bridges

When Geography ended, Cody stood behind his chair and stretched. Then he paced the length of his row, getting some exercise before sitting through another hour-long class. A group of students walked in. Their voices were raised in excitement. One girl waved her hands in the air as she described a fire that had started in her Speech class.

Cody's stomach plummeted. Odds were that that was Dacia's class. He focused on the girl, listening intently to everything she said.

"Blue flames shot up off of Cassandra's desk." Her shudder was exaggerated. "It was terrifying."

Cody grabbed his things and darted out into the hallway, sprinting through the front door. Dacia didn't have class for another hour. He looked around the buildings trying to guess where she would go.

The library.

It would be quiet there, and she could hide from everybody in one of the cubicles. As he raced across the green space, gray clouds, heavy with rain gathered above him.

If he hadn't been sure before, he would've been after seeing them.

She'd gone a week with no incidents, and he'd begun to think that Phlox would be the new start she had been hoping for.

He stepped inside Krummholz Library and looked around, wondering where she would be. He finally found her sitting in a cubicle as far from the door as she could. Her elbows were propped on the desk, and she held her head in her hands.

Walking toward her, he tried to figure out what to say. He'd seen her do some amazing things over the years but never anything like this.

He remembered the day he'd been so excited to tell his parents what he'd seen. He thought the bus would never get to his stop. He'd sprinted from the top of the driveway and through the front door.

"Mom!" He'd kicked his shoes off and dashed through the house, searching for her. He'd finally found her in the garden, plucking ripe tomatoes off their vines. He'd darted into the yard, forgetting he was only in his socks. Rocks poked into his feet, but he didn't care. This was too important. "Mom," he shouted, unable to contain his excitement.

She'd looked up, smiling broadly at him while brushing her hair back. "Cody, where are your shoes?"

"Not now." He skidded to a halt. "Gotta tell you something."

"What do you *need* to tell me?" She grabbed the bucket of tomatoes and started walking toward the house.

He followed her. "You know my friend Dacia." He didn't wait for her to respond. "She's magic! At recess, Brianna was teasing her."

"What did she say?" His mom held the door open, and he'd gone inside.

"That she was stupid." He clenched his hands into tight fists. "That she was an only child because her parents learned from their mistakes."

His mom gasped. "How cruel."

"Blue fire came out of Dacia's fingers." His words had sped up, crashing into each other. "It was awesome! Brianna was so scared." He hadn't told his parents the first time that he'd seen her use her magic. That time, he had been terrified.

His mom had lifted one eyebrow. "Are you sure about that, Cody?" She'd ruffled his hair. "People aren't magic."

His dad had said the same thing when he got home from work, but Cody knew what he had seen, and he believed.

Thinking back on it, Cody knew why it had upset Dacia so much. At the time, he hadn't known her brother had died in the house fire that brought her family to Bittersweet.

"Dacia." He kept his voice quiet, hoping nobody else would realize they were back here. When he put his hand on her shoulder, she jumped. "Oops. Sorry to scare you." He chuckled. "Guess you didn't hear me."

She stared up into his eyes, not saying anything at all. Finally, she shook her head.

He wondered what had been going through her mind but didn't ask. "So … the fire." He squatted in front of her and put his hands on her knees. He needed to touch her, to know she was okay. "Yours?"

She lowered her head. "Yep."

"No biggie." His thumb ached to caress her leg, but he fought the urge, holding perfectly still. "Nobody knows but me, and I won't tell."

A tear raced down her cheek and dripped off her chin. "Cassandra knew. She told me she'd get even with me." Another tear followed.

He opened his mouth, but nothing came out.

"I thought things would be better when I got out of Bittersweet. I thought I would be able to blend in here. Now, I'm not so sure." She turned away from him, and he left his hands in the air where they had been, feeling her absence. "Samantha will find out. What will she think of me?"

"Hey, don't start feeling sorry for yourself." His voice was rough, and when she snapped her head toward him, he realized she thought he was scolding her.

Anger flashed through her emerald eyes. "Why shouldn't I?"

"I like sunshine, and it'd be nice not to walk in rain."

She lifted her eyes to the ceiling and let out a long breath. Her hair tumbled over the back of the chair, and he had to look away from the column of her neck. "You're just jealous."

He turned back just as she looked at him and raised his eyebrows. "Jealous?"

"Yeah, you wish your moods could change the weather."

"Darn right, I do." He pulled her to her feet and slung her backpack over his shoulder.

As they strolled across campus, Cody stuffed one hand into his pocket and held the strap of Dacia's bag with his other. It wasn't raining, but the clouds that had rolled in covered the sky.

He sat beside her in the classroom and watched her as she stared at the door.

"Dacia, breathe." Cody threw his arm over the back of her chair. "Relax."

She shook her head. "Can't."

Wondering what had possessed him to put it there anyway, he pulled his arm away and ripped a piece of paper from his notebook. "Tic-Tac-Toe?"

She marked a quick "X" in the upper left-hand corner. Three moves later, she said, "You let me win."

He shrugged. "It's working."

He saw when Cassandra and her friends entered the room, but he continued playing the game with Dacia, hoping she wouldn't notice.

Unfortunately, Cassandra stopped right behind Dacia, standing over her. Through gritted teeth, she said, "You should have been drowned the day you were born."

Cody had been raised never to harm a girl, but he wanted to push Cassandra down the stairs. It took everything he had in him to stay in his seat. When Dacia started to stand, he reached his hand out and covered her fist with it. Not thinking, he rubbed his thumb over hers. The movement sent a pang of desire racing through him, but he didn't stop. She needed him right now, and the motion seemed to calm her.

Cassandra looked from Cody's hand to his face and shook her head. "You could do so much better." She flipped her hair. "If you want to try, call me."

He squeezed Dacia's hand. "Nah, she's the best."

"What. Ever." Cassandra turned and stomped up the stairs.

Cody bent toward Dacia, and her scent washed over him, a combination of vanilla and roses. He breathed her in for a moment before whispering, "You have to ignore her."

She looked up at him from the corner of her eyes and rubbed her arms. "Now, that's a power I'd love to have."

Chapter 3
Seeking Advice

Cody slouched against his Camaro. Dacia's roommate, Samantha said that Dacia had been called to the dean's office. When it started storming in the middle of an otherwise gorgeous day, he knew there would be a chance that Dacia would need him.

She climbed into the passenger seat without as much as a hello. Cody followed and started the car. The radio blared. He reached over and turned it down, still on but too quiet to be distracting. "Where to?"

"Away." She stared out the window as he drove.

He tapped on the wheel. "Well?"

"Dean Aspen knows."

He stayed quiet, waiting for her to continue, not wanting to push her.

"She saw."

The car slowed down, and Cody pulled onto an overlook. A break in the trees left a view of the mountains with meadows and a river flowing through the valley below.

Dacia turned toward Cody. Her eyebrows pinched together in confusion. "Why are you stopping?"

He tilted his head to the side and watched her. He wanted to reach across the console and smooth out the wrinkled skin between her eyes. Would she like it? Would she reject him? He let out a sigh. "This doesn't sound like a conversation we should have while I'm driving."

She chewed on her lip. "I needed privacy."

"Yeah. I get that." Needing to focus his attention on something besides her lips, he turned the radio off. "You make it rain?"

She nodded.

"Stopped my basketball game, but didn't last long."
"Nah."

He ran his hands over the steering wheel. "So … not all bad."

Her lips pulled up into an imitation of a smile. "Not all bad but …" She let out a troubled sigh. "It can't be good, can it?"

Cody reached over and squeezed her hand. "Start at the beginning."

She leaned her head back, stared up at the ceiling, and told him about her meeting with Dean Aspen. "She asked me about the fire. I denied everything, but then—" she sucked in a deep breath "—the room started shaking. I thought for sure she'd kick me out, but she offered to train me to control whatever this is."

"So, where's the dilemma? Let her help you."

She glared at him. "The dilemma. Really, you don't see it?" She tugged her fingers through her hair. "She knows what I can do."

"So do I." He kept his voice calm and even.

"So do Mom and Dad."

He could see the hurt in her eyes even though she tried to cover it with anger. He waved his hand through the air.

"They can't stand to be around me. They're scared and in denial." She slumped forward, dropping her head into her hands. "And I can't even blame them."

Dark clouds rolled in, crashing against each other, creating lightning that spider-webbed overhead. Thunder emphasized the storm's anger.

"Dacia." He kept his voice soft, not wanting to rile her. "The storm of the century won't help."

Dacia got out, slammed the door shut, and paced.

Knowing that she needed her space, Cody watched her for a couple of minutes before he unbuckled his seatbelt and slowly stepped out. He leaned against his car, his arms folded over his chest, and watched her steps lose their aggressiveness. When the sky looked less foreboding, he said, "Don't overreact."

She spun on her heel, and the look she shot him would've cowed lesser men.

If looks could kill, he thought. "Samantha needs to know."

"Why?"

"Really?" He walked over, hands in his pockets, not meeting her gaze. She wouldn't hurt him, but he didn't want to antagonize her. "How do you want her to find out? With you in control or not?"

She turned back around and kicked a rock, sending it soaring over the road and down the hill. "But, how am I supposed to tell her? She won't understand. No one does."

"I do," he said softly. "So does Dean Aspen."

The anger seemed to drain out of her. "She wasn't even scared."

He swallowed hard, not quite sure what to say. "That's good, isn't it?"

"No." She took a long, slow breath. "It doesn't make sense."

He closed the distance between them and squeezed her shoulder. "It doesn't scare me."

"The first time?"

He chuckled, but it was humorless. The first time he'd seen blue flames burst from her fingertips was just a couple of months after he'd met her. They were riding their bikes home from school when a dog jumped its fence and chased after them. Pedaling as hard as they could, it still gained on them. Dacia had stopped and turned around. She lifted her hands, and fire danced over her palm. She'd thrown it down between them, and the dog ran away yipping. "Yeah, terrified."

She pulled away from him and stared at the distant mountains. "I don't know if I can trust her. What if she wants to use me somehow?"

Cody sat on a bench outside Cacomistle Hall. He spread his arms over the back of it and stretched his feet out in front of him. With his head tilted toward the sky, he closed his eyes and waited.

He heard her walk over. When her shadow settled over him, he said, "What'd she say?"

"How did you know it was me?"

He pulled his eyebrows together and looked up at her. Did he dare tell her that he recognized her vanilla and roses scent or that he'd long ago memorized the sound of her gait? "Who else would it be?"

"Anybody."

He didn't answer. There was nothing he could say without giving away his feelings for her.

She plopped down on the bench next to him. "She believes we are part of a prophecy, and I'm supposed to save the world." She slumped back and chewed her lower lip.

If that was true, it explained her magic. It was an explanation he could get behind. He nodded. "Cool."

"It's not cool." She smacked his arm and laughed. "The only other person who accepts me is a lunatic."

He sat up and pulled his arms in to prevent himself from sliding one over her shoulders. "If she can help, let her."

"I know. I told her I would, but … she believes in a prophecy. How can I take her seriously?"

Cody stood and stretched. "One step at a time, Dacia."

"What?" Her confusion threw him off. She shook her head like she was clearing it and said, "Oh, yeah."

He held his hand out, and when she slipped hers into it, he pulled her to her feet. "Maybe there's a reason you're the way you are. Maybe you have a destiny."

"Uh-huh. Sure."

"You never know."

Chapter 4

Hoping For The Best

The jiggle of the key in the doorknob made the air whoosh from Dacia's lungs.

Cody knelt on the floor in front of her and rested his hands on hers. "Breathe, Dacia. It's all right. Even if she can't accept it, you've got me. I won't abandon you."

"I know you won't, Code." She squeezed his fingers.

Samantha opened the door. "Hey, guys. Give me a few minutes, and we can head out."

Reluctantly releasing Dacia's hands, Cody stood up. "We're going to order pizza and stay here … more privacy."

"Oh." Samantha set her stuff down and sat in the yellow chair that Dacia had affectionately named Big Bird. "So … uh, what's going on? This sounds serious."

Cody sat on the arm of Cookie Monster, the blue chair, and rested his hand on Dacia's shoulder. He closed his eyes and swallowed hard. He was finding too many excuses to touch her lately. Maybe it was because they were away from home, and his brothers weren't around to torment him. Maybe it was because of the way other guys looked at her, and he was afraid she would look back. Every time he touched her, it got more difficult to let go.

"We haven't known each other very long." Dacia's voice quivered.

"Yeah …" Samantha trailed off, and she grimaced.

Dacia lowered her head and took a deep breath. "Remember the day Cassandra's books caught on fire?"

"Uh, yeah." Samantha pinched her eyebrows together and tilted her head to the side. "It's the most exciting thing that's happened here. What about it?"

Cody stood up, and Dacia's chair rocked back and forth from the force of it. He couldn't let Dacia do this unless he knew for certain Samantha would keep her secret. "Can Dacia trust you?" His feet were hip-width apart, his arms crossed over his chest, and he stared down at her. Intimidation wasn't something he normally did, but for Dacia, he'd try it.

Samantha looked from him to Dacia. "What's this about?"

"Can. She. Trust. You?" he asked again with more force. If Samantha was going to hate one of them, he'd rather it was him.

"Yes, she can." She rolled her eyes at him.

Cody plopped down on the arm of Dacia's chair, bringing the rocking to a stop. "Go ahead then."

"I did it," Dacia said before covering her face with her hands.

Samantha tipped her head to the side and looked between the two of them. "Did what?"

"Set her books on fire." Dacia's voice got higher pitched with every word.

Samantha laughed, and the sound was forced. "Sure. How? You were on the stage, nowhere near her."

"I didn't mean to, but sometimes I have trouble controlling my emotions. I'm not …" Dacia's voice faltered, and she dragged a shaking hand through her hair.

Cody watched, wishing there was some way he could comfort her. Wishing he could help.

"I'm not normal."

Samantha glanced between them, backing away slightly as she did. "I don't know what you're saying."

Seeing the defeat on Dacia's face, Cody squeezed her shoulder. This had been his idea. Maybe he shouldn't have put Dacia through it. He'd seen what had happened when her powers surfaced around other people. He knew that not everyone could accept her for what she was. "Let me."

Dacia nodded and slumped down.

"Dacia has powers." Even though he was talking to Samantha, he never took his eyes off of Dacia. "I guess that's the word for what she can do. When she gets overemotional, it rains." He pointed at the window. He hadn't looked outside, but since Samantha's return, the room had grown noticeably darker. "It's clouding up now. If she's angry, things fly through the air or catch on fire. Dean Aspen is helping her learn control."

"Um … okaaay. Sure." A hollow laugh penetrated the air. "You had me going for a minute." She slid her eyes from Dacia's face to Cody's. "So, what's really going on?"

"It's the truth." Dacia's voice was more desperate than he could ever remember hearing it.

Samantha twirled her bracelet around her wrist. "Yeah, well I suppose it could happen." She forced a smile at us. "According to Mom, I can breathe fire when I want."

Dacia ran her fingers through her hair. "I knew you wouldn't believe me."

"Okay." Samantha threw her arms up and stood. "So, make me believe … show me."

"I can't." Dacia held Samantha's gaze for a few seconds before looking down.

"You can't …" Samantha's voice was a challenge. "Why not?"

Dacia wrung her hands together, then wiped them down her legs. "I don't have that kind of control."

"So, let me get this straight. You have these mysterious"—Samantha made air quotes around the words as she said them—"powers, but you have no control of them. Is that right?"

"Basically."

Samantha crossed her arms over her chest and pinned Cody with a steely gaze. "Besides the clouds—which I don't see how you can be sure Dacia is responsible for—have you seen these powers manifested?"

He returned the same hard look. "Yeah, I have, and … well, the first time it was scary as hell."

"Funny … very funny." Tears brightened her eyes. She obviously thought they were joking and had taken it too far. "Do you really think this is amusing? Because I sure don't."

Cody felt bad for her, but for Dacia's sake, they needed her to believe. He pulled himself up and stepped toward her. "No, it's not funny. It's Dacia's life. Believe it or not, it's the way it is."

"It's fine." Dacia had pulled her legs onto the chair and was curled over them, making her appear smaller than she already was.

Samantha turned her piercing gaze on Dacia. "It's not fine. We haven't known each other long enough for the two of you to gang up on me. It's one thing to joke around but another to keep going." She pointed her finger at Dacia. "I thought you were my friend."

"I am."

"Then stop yanking my chain!"

Dacia planted her feet on the floor and dug her fingernails into the arms of her chair. "I am not. Yanking. Your chain."

The walls trembled, and Samantha's backpack wobbled before falling over and spilling its contents. The TV shuddered on its stand. Samantha's eyes widened, and her hand covered her mouth.

Cody stood in front of Dacia and held her gaze with his. "Calm down, Dacia." He brushed his fingers over her cheek.

Samantha looked at the door, then back at Cody and Dacia. "I think I need a minute."

Cody's heart plummeted. He stared at the door, not wanting to face Dacia. This had been his idea, and he'd been wrong.

Turning slowly, he said, "Didn't see that coming." He looked down, focusing on her hands. He couldn't bear to see the pain in her eyes, knowing he was the one who had put it there. "I'm sorry."

"I knew this would happen." Her voice was flat and lifeless. "But, I hoped it wouldn't."

"She wasn't screaming." He wanted to be positive for her. He wanted things to work out even though they were looking grim. "Could be a good sign."

"You know there's not always a pot of gold at the end of the rainbow, don't you?" She stared out the window for a moment, then added, "Sometimes there isn't even a rainbow."

Cody reached his hand down. It shook, but she didn't seem to notice. "There's always the possibility of a rainbow." He tugged her to her feet. "Let's get some fresh air. Maybe look for rainbows."

When Cody opened the door, Samantha fell back into his arms and let out a scream of surprise. Red tinged her cheeks as she tried to right herself.

She didn't run away, Cody thought as he steadied her. "Didn't make it far."

"No." Samantha tucked a lock of hair behind her ear. "I just needed a second."

Dacia stumbled and bent forward, resting her hands on her knees. "So, you're okay with this?"

"Uh … well …"

Samantha walked back into the room and plopped down hard enough to rock the chair. "No, I can't wrap my mind around this. There's got to be some logical explanation, something that makes sense."

"There isn't." Dacia wiped her hands on her jeans, drawing Cody's attention to her.

His gaze traveled from her freckled cheeks to her toes, lingering as he took in every bit of her. He shook his head and turned away. He'd known her since he was seven. Why were these feelings suddenly so overpowering?

"Believe me, I wish there was." Dacia looked down at her feet. They had talked at length about her powers. Cody knew that she felt like a freak. He knew that she hated them, hated that they made her an anomaly. "I wish there were other people like me, so I didn't feel so alone all the time."

Samantha's soft brown eyes searched Cody's face, then Dacia's as if she was looking for some sign of deception. "Okay, so you set Cassandra's books on fire. What does that have to do with Dean Aspen?"

Dacia sat down, playing with her hair as she did. "When she talked to me Tuesday, she caught a glimpse of my powers."

Samantha's fingers shot up to her mouth to cover her gasp. "Oh, no."

"Oh, yeah." Dacia nodded. "And, she was excited."

"She was?"

"Yeah, she thinks I'm part of a prophecy."

Samantha's mouth fell open, and she stared at Dacia. "So … Dean Aspen is crazy?"

A surprised laugh burst from Dacia's lips. "It kinda seems that way."

Cody was thrilled that Samantha had come to her senses, but he needed her to understand. He crossed his arms over his chest. His posture was stiff, imposing. His voice was hard. "You, Dean Aspen, and I are the only ones who know what Dacia can do. Cassandra is just guessing."

Samantha swallowed. "Okay?"

"Needs to stay that way."

She glared at him, then turned to Dacia. "Dacia, you can call your guard dog off. I'm not going to tell anyone."

Cody rubbed his hands together and thanked his lucky stars. He hadn't led Dacia astray. "So that's done. What kinda pizza we gettin'?"

Chapter 5

Power Unparalleled

Cody woke up with a start. Sweat covered his chest and blankets. He stared up at the ceiling and let the nightmare replay through his memories, knowing he couldn't stop it if he tried.

Dacia had been wandering campus on her own again. Something, a noise, a feeling, a smell, whatever it had been startled her, and she stopped. She turned ever so slowly, almost like she was fighting against it but couldn't quite keep herself from looking. When she saw whatever it was, her eyes widened. The color drained from her face, and she let out a shrill, terrified scream.

Cody thought she would never move. Her body seemed frozen, but then she turned and sprinted away.

Whatever was behind her was faster, though. Knowing she couldn't outrun it, she darted to the side and hid.

"Come out and face your death." The creature roared. The sound was like a loud clap of thunder on a clear day.

What would have happened if the unexpected bellow wouldn't have woken him? Would he have watched Dacia die again? It had been one thing to have these nightmares before he'd known her, but now that she was a part of his life, he couldn't stomach the thought of witnessing her death.

He rolled over and looked at the clock. 4:03. The red lights sneered at him, taunting him, knowing he couldn't go back to sleep after the nightmare he'd had.

Not wanting to wake up his roommate, Drew, Cody lay in bed and did the only thing he could. He thought.

He had classes and homework. He missed his parents, his three younger brothers, and his baby sister, but his thoughts went to Dacia.

He remembered her sitting in her blue, fuzzy chair. Her red hair was a striking contrast to it. He might have been distracted by her beauty if there hadn't been so much fear in her green eyes. She'd had a lesson with Dean Aspen that day and had asked what the prophecy was.

Sarah had gone on to tell her that she would have to fight a demon. One that returned from the Abyss every 999 years in the hopes of finally defeating the chosen one. It sounded a bit far-fetched to him, but even though Dacia played it off, he could tell that part of her believed it.

His nightmare, though, made him wonder. Could the creature that had been chasing her be the demon she feared? Could it be real?

He rolled onto his side and tried to think of other things, but his thoughts kept circling back to Dacia.

For the last few weeks, he had been walking her to and from her lessons with Sarah. Cassandra, Bryce, Alvin, and Vanessa, dubbed the Potato Heads by Dacia and Samantha, had been trying to catch Dacia alone. If Cody had any say in it, she would never step foot outside of her door without him with her.

Since they were seven years old, he had felt like it was his duty to protect her, and he doubted anything would ever happen that would prevent him from trying to keep her safe.

Because of the Potato Heads, he dropped Dacia off for her lessons, then made sure he was back to get her before she could even think about leaving on her own. While he wasn't sure if she was learning anything that could help her defeat a demon, if it came to that, he had noticed that she had fewer accidents. As far as he knew, she hadn't lost control of her powers since she'd frozen Cassandra's hands in the bathroom sink, and there were fewer un-forecasted storms.

When his alarm went off, he threw the covers back and got out of bed. He was sick of lying there, staring at the ceiling. He grabbed his clothes and was almost out the door when Drew said, "Going to see your hot girlfriend?"

"Dude"—Cody turned around, shaking his head—"how many times do I have to tell you we're just friends."

Drew snorted. "Sure. Is that why you got so angry when I said I was going to ask her out?"

Cody pinched his eyes shut. The thought of seeing her with another guy ate him up inside, but he knew it would happen someday. She was smart, funny, beautiful, and there was no way he was the only one who saw it. "She's too good for you."

"No doubt." Drew stood up and stretched his arms over his head. "I imagine you think you're the only one good enough for her."

Cody dragged his hand through his hair, hoping to get it to lay down before he walked out into the hall. "She doesn't want me."

"Have you asked her what she wants?" Drew raised an eyebrow and picked up a shirt off the floor, smelling it before pulling it over his head.

Cody pulled the door open, and right before leaving, he said, "No."

While Dacia was in her lesson, Cody sat in one of the empty rooms of Cacomistle Hall and worked on his homework. Nobody stopped by to see if he wanted to play video games or basketball or grab something to eat, so he actually was able to get it done. He pulled his phone out of his pocket and tapped the screen to check the time. That was about all it was good for these days. Phlox University was a dead zone for cell phones, but he didn't mind. It was nice to get a break from the constant bombardment of texts, messages, and social media.

Time to get Dacia. He shoved his things into his bag and jogged up the open staircase. Not wanting to look too eager, he slowed to a walk and sauntered into Dean Aspen's office.

Dacia had her back to him, facing the magnificent view of the Snowfire Mountains. "I can't say it's something I want to do. But, at least I have good friends to try to help me through it."

He was glad she could say that. For as long as he'd known her, friendship hadn't come easy to Dacia. He didn't know what fate had put her with Samantha as a roommate, but he would forever be grateful to it. "Especially me." He smiled. "You okay, Dean? You look pale."

"I'm fine, Cody, and please call me Sarah," she said, not managing to hide the stress in her voice. "I'm worried about Dacia, but I think she might have a little more strength than I've given her credit for."

He stood behind the couch and looked down at Dacia. "Yeah, she's pretty tough."

"Why don't you two get out of here and try to enjoy the rest of the day?" Sarah smiled, a forced expression that didn't reach her hazel eyes.

Dacia scrambled to her feet, grabbing her bag and slinging it over her shoulder. "That sounds like a great idea."

"I'll see you Tuesday, Dacia," Sarah said as Cody and Dacia headed out the door. "Unless, of course, something happens before then that you think I should know about."

They walked down the stairs next to each other, not feeling the need to talk. When they stepped outside, Cody breathed in the fresh mountain air. There was nothing else quite like it for alleviating stress. They strolled down the sidewalk for a bit before he asked, "So, how was your lesson?"

"It went pretty well. I controlled my powers, and nothing even flew at Sarah." She straightened her shoulders, standing a little taller, and a wide grin spread across her face.

God, she was beautiful. "Great!" He looked away from her as Drew's words ran through his mind, *Have you asked her what she wants?*

She didn't say any more for quite a while, but he caught her looking up at his face several times. Knowing she would tell him when she was ready, he waited patiently.

"Sarah tried to use you against me to get some sort of reaction."

"Why?" Cody stopped walking and frowned down at Dacia. *How could Sarah think he would harm Dacia?* "I'd never hurt you."

"I know you wouldn't." She patted his arm. "She tried to make me believe you were Cassandra's boyfriend. She must think we're more than friends …" She looked away before he could glean anything from her expression. "I guess she was trying to make me jealous."

Cody's face reddened, and he stared into the distance. "Did it work?" he asked without looking at her.

"I held my own."

He turned toward her and raised a single questioning eyebrow.

She didn't give him any indication that she knew what he meant. "I asked her if she knows anything more about Nefarious than what she told me at our first meeting."

"And?"

"She told me he has the power to gain the allegiance of humans, so not only do I have to worry about defeating him, I might have to fight people, too." She seemed to shrink a little.

Cody put his hand on her shoulder. He wanted to pull her against him and wrap her in his arms. He wanted to protect her from this, but if there was a demon out there, he didn't know how he could keep her safe. "It'll be all right, Dacia. Know it doesn't seem like it, but things'll work out. Samantha and I will help you any way we can." He set his jaw, determined to protect her. "You know I won't let anything or anyone hurt you."

"Yeah, I know you'll do your best to keep anything from happening to me." She slid her hand into his.

Warmth spread through his fingertips and up his arm. *Get a grip. Seriously.*

"But I don't know if you'll be able to protect me this time, Cody."

They walked in silence for a while, both of them uneasy. "Sarah also told me unicorns, fairies, and other magical beasts exist. She told me she has seen some of them, too."

Cody cocked his head. "You believe her?"

"I don't know—" she paused and looked up at him with a raised eyebrow "—but, how can I deny they're real when I believe in a fantasy that includes a horrific beast?"

"Touché." He squeezed her fingers. "Wouldn't mind seeing one."

"Me either."

Chapter 6
What Next?

Dacia, Samantha, and Cody hiked through the timber behind the dorms to Falcon Lake. The path was surrounded by thick woods that waited patiently for their chance to encroach on the dirt. Roots and rocks jutted up through the ground, creating tripping hazards, and low-hanging branches poked at trespassers.

"I really should be reading a book for English Lit." Dacia pushed a branch out of the way, knocking free an orange leaf. It swirled through the air, drifting to the ground where several others littered the forest floor. "I have a book report to do, but I don't think I could concentrate on it today anyway."

"Sounds like you." Samantha tripped on a root but caught herself before she fell. "I suppose it's due Friday, and you'll read the book and write the report Thursday."

"Giving her too much credit, Sam." Cody chuckled. "Won't be done 'til class Friday."

"Well, for your information, the report is due Wednesday," Dacia said in the snootiest voice Cody had ever heard her use. "I guess that makes both of you wrong. You know I'll get it done. I always do."

"You'll finish Wednesday morning then," Cody said.

She smacked his arm with the back of her hand. "I'm going to finish it before then just to prove the two of you wrong!"

Cody rubbed his chin. "Pay for dinner Friday if you finish before Wednesday." He knew that Dacia worked harder when someone bet against her, and he knew he would be the one paying, but it would be worth it to get to spend the evening with her.

After nearly a mile, they stepped from the path. Pine trees clung to the rocks surrounding Falcon Lake, growing to impossible heights. Picnic tables and a park were sprinkled around the stunning blue water with a playground between a few of them.

They tossed their things on top of one of the tables and walked toward the shore. For the first few feet, you could see every rock through the crystal-clear water. After that, the bottom dropped out, and the lake deepened to a dark, navy blue.

While Samantha and Dacia sat on boulders gazing at the scenery. Cody picked up the flattest rocks he could find and skipped them across the surface. When all his stones were gone, they decided to play Frisbee. Dacia threw it to Cody, so he tossed it to Samantha. Then Samantha flung it over Dacia's head every time. Cody noticed Dacia's frustration rising, but he had always thought of her like a kitten or a lion cub when she was angry. Too cute to be menacing.

"Samantha, I'm here. I'm five foot five inches tall, not seven feet. Please throw it to me!" Dacia's hands emphasized each of her words.

Samantha's face immediately turned bright red. "I'm sorry, Dacia. I've never been good at this."

The next time Samantha threw it, Dacia jumped.

Cody went as still as a statue, except for his mouth dropping open. He stared at Dacia catching the Frisbee while hanging three feet above the ground.

"What?" Dacia stepped forward to throw the Frisbee, apparently not realizing that she was flying. When her foot didn't touch anything but air, she flung her arms out and plummeted.

Cody sprinted toward her, hoping to catch her before she hit the ground, but he was too late. Her arms flailed, and her legs kicked out in front of her. She landed on the hard-packed dirt with a thump.

"Nice hang time!" Cody reached down to her, hoping she'd only hurt her pride.

Her eyes darted around before she grabbed his hand and let him pull her to her feet. "Thank God there weren't too many people around." She tugged on her bottom lip with her teeth. "That would've been hard to explain."

"How did you do that, Dacia?" Samantha's mouth hung open, and her eyes were wide.

"I was frustrated." Dacia wiped dirt off the back of her jeans. "I didn't want to chase the Frisbee again. I leapt and all that emotion must have …" She pulled her fingers through her curls. "I don't know … given me a boost."

Knowing these things made her self-conscious, Cody shrugged it off, acting like it was no big deal. "Wonder what else you can do."

"I wish—" she picked up the Frisbee and flipped it over in her hands "—I knew how to make myself do these things instead of them just happening to me."

Samantha shot her a shaky smile. "You'll figure it out."

"I've had powers all my life." Dacia folded her arms over her chest and leered at the ground. "I haven't figured anything out."

Thunder rumbled as storm clouds gathered in the sky. Dacia took a deep breath, walked to a picnic table, and sat. She stared out at Falcon Lake, watching the wind make ripples dance across the water.

Cody sat next to her. He lifted his hand, wanting to pull her against his side and comfort her, but she dodged it.

"I need a few minutes." She rubbed her hand down her face. "If you don't mind."

Cody hunched his shoulders and tried to smile at her, but it felt forced and wrong. She had always run to him when she had problems, but this time she was pushing him away. "Uh, sure. I'll hang with Samantha."

He walked away, wondering if he'd done something wrong, if he'd come on too strongly lately, or if she just didn't need him the way she used to. What if she was moving on but he was staying stagnant?

Cody and Samantha strolled along the lake for a while. Most everyone else had left when the storm clouds rolled in. They walked until the blue skies returned. Then they sat at one of the other picnic tables.

"You know her better than I do." Samantha looked over at Dacia. She was still staring out at the water. Her hair blew around her face, but she didn't seem to mind. "Is she going to be okay?"

Cody rested his elbows on the table and held his head in his hands. "Hope so. She's doing better most days." They looked toward Dacia, and she waved them over.

"Well, what did you two decide?" she asked as they approached the table. "How are you going to make things better, or did you decide I'm a lost cause?"

Samantha smiled. "You know we decided a long time ago that you're a lost cause."

When Dacia didn't say anything, Samantha added, "Actually, we decided it's about dinner time, so do you want to eat here or go?"

"All we have here are snacks." Dacia pointed at the backpack on the end of the table.

Cody rubbed his stomach. "I could go for a bacon cheeseburger and fries."

Samantha went over to her bag and pulled out a pen and paper. "Why don't you two tell me what you want? I'll go back and order it while you get all of our stuff rounded up."

"That works." Cody reached into his pocket and threw some bills down in front of Samantha. "Bacon cheeseburger, lettuce, tomato, mayo, and cheddar fries. Dacia?"

"I'll have the same, hold the mayo."

Samantha patted Dacia on the back before heading toward the trail. She looked like she had wanted to say something but didn't know what to say or how to say it.

Cody watched her disappear into the trees before he sat down next to Dacia. He reached for her hand, hoping she wouldn't pull away this time. When she didn't, he relaxed a little. "You okay?"

"I'll be fine." With the hand he wasn't holding onto, she pulled her hair out from under her shirt, flipping it over her collar. "I'm sorry I sent you away. I needed a little space."

Cody stared into her emerald eyes. They looked so sad, and he wondered if there was any way to take her pain. "Don't apologize. Sometimes you need space. Sometimes you need me."

"Thanks, Cody." She leaned her head against his shoulder, and his heart sped up in response. "I have no idea what I'd do without you."

"You'd be lost." He rested his head on hers, wondering how she felt about him, wondering if she would say yes if he asked her to be his.

"There's more truth to that than you realize."

Her words gave him hope. Butterflies flew through him. Their flapping wings beat against his stomach walls, making it impossible for him to stay seated. "Let's sit by the water." He stood and reached for her hand. When she slipped hers into it, his courage grew. He would do this. He would ask her. "Take a while for our food to get there."

They sat on a massive boulder at the edge of the lake. Cody's insides trembled worse than the ground during an avalanche while he debated on what exactly to say to her. He reached over, put his arm around her shoulders, and pulled her closer. *Now or never.* He released a deep breath, steadying himself. "I've, uh, been thinking about Sarah using me and Cassandra to make you jealous."

She tilted her head back so she could look up at him. "Okay?" She was perfectly kissable with her mouth angled toward him like that.

Not wanting to scare her away, he focused on the lake. "Thought about it. More than once."

"Cody, I never expected you to ask me out." There was a slight hitch in her voice, but he didn't know if that was a good thing or a bad thing.

He cleared his throat, hoping he wouldn't sound husky when he talked again. "You're my best friend. Don't wanna lose you."

She slipped her arm around his back, and there was a long pause before she said, "Friendship's good."

Cody's heart plummeted. He'd never felt anything quite like it before. He was utterly humiliated, but he didn't want her to know it. He just kept staring at the sun sinking over Falcon Lake. After a few seconds or an eternity, he wasn't sure which, Dacia laid her head on his shoulder.

He closed his eyes and focused on keeping his breathing even. How could she sit here like this, but not want anything more than friendship? Didn't she know he was dying inside?

"Are you ready to go back?" She gazed at him, but he couldn't turn to look at her. He couldn't let her see his eyes. She would know how hurt he was, and he didn't want that. He didn't want to push her away. He couldn't lose her. "I imagine Samantha wonders what happened to us."

"Nah." Cody squeezed her arm gently. "Told her we needed to talk."

They sat there until the shadows lengthened, and the sunset was little more than an orange glow on the horizon. When stars dotted the sky and she couldn't read him like an open book, he stood up. Then he helped her to her feet. They walked toward the trail, and he realized his mistake. The path back to Phlox University was unlit.

"I guess I should've packed a flashlight," Dacia said what Cody was thinking.

Helping guide each other through the woods, they held hands. Cody focused on where he placed each foot, trying to keep Dacia from tripping over rocks or roots. He almost didn't realize she was trying to get his attention when she nudged him.

"What?" he whispered.

Her words were so soft that if the wind blew, he was sure they would be whisked away. "Somebody's hiding behind those trees."

He pulled her off the trail and slowly led her through the timber. Their eyes adjusted well enough to see the tree trunks and larger branches, but the ground was another story. Twigs snapped beneath their feet. They crept forward, making it past the spot where Dacia had seen the shadows, but if someone had been there, they were long gone.

Stopping, they searched the darkness for any sign of people. They were about to start walking again when a branch snapped. Cody's grip on Dacia's hand tightened.

The shadows in front of them grew darker as someone stepped into them. Dacia took a step back and stifled a scream. Cody looked over his shoulder just as somebody said, "Nice of you to step off of the path where nobody can see you."

"What do you want, Bryce?" Cody relaxed a little. He had played basketball with Bryce several times since school started. They weren't friends, but there was no animosity between them.

"We'll do the talking here." Alvin Leach's voice came from behind them.

"The freak here"—Bryce pointed at Dacia—"needs to stay away from Cassandra. If she doesn't, she'll answer to us."

"I've been trying to stay away from her since I got here, so that won't be a problem on my part!" Dacia's voice rose with each word she said. "Now, why don't you move outta the way?"

Bryce stuck his face right in front of Dacia's. "We'll be keeping our eyes on you, Freak. You'd better watch your back." He pushed his fingers into her shoulder.

"Back away from her. Now." Cody's voice turned dark and dangerous, protective.

Bryce turned slightly, looking like he was going to walk away. Instead, he swung around and punched Cody in the jaw.

Cody never saw it coming. He stumbled backward, catching himself before falling to the ground. He spat at Bryce's feet, then held onto his jaw, moving it from side to side, making sure it still worked like it was supposed to.

A tingly, aching sensation spread through his cheek as he regained his bearings and pulled his fist back.

"Go ahead, Cody, hit him," Alvin hissed. "You can't get us both at the same time."

Cody turned his head to get a better look at Alvin and was lowering his fist when Bryce threw another punch at him. It didn't land on Cody's face. It stopped about an inch away, and Bryce howled in pain.

Dacia grabbed Cody's hand, and they ran through the trees, stumbling and fighting their way back onto the path. They sprinted until the campus lights illuminated them. Bryce's screams followed them all of the way back to the dorms.

Panting, they stepped into the glow of the lamps.

"What'd you do to Bryce?" Cody asked as soon as he caught his breath.

"I have no idea." Dacia sucked in a breath. "I couldn't let him hit you again. He should've hit me."

"No." Cody clenched his hands at his sides. Just the thought of one of them striking her made him want to punch something. He looked at the light pole but knew it would hurt him more than he would hurt it.

"I'm the one he has a problem with."

"If he'd hit you, more than just his hand would hurt," Cody spoke with a fierceness he rarely possessed. "Didn't hit him 'cause couldn't bear to see you get hurt. If you'd've gotten hit, all bets woulda been off."

She set her hand on his shoulder as if she knew it was the one thing that could calm him. "Stop worrying about me. I can handle myself."

"I'll never stop worrying about you." He took hold of her hand and led her to the dorm. "Know you can handle yourself, but know you'd never forgive yourself if you took it too far."

When Dacia opened the door, Samantha spun around. "Where have you been? I thought something hap—" Her voice broke off when she saw them. "Cody, are you all right? You look like you've been in a fight."

"Fine and sort of." Cody summed everything up quickly, then said, "Let's eat!"

"That's all you're going to tell me?" Samantha sounded a little wounded about not getting the full story. "How did Dacia save you?"

"We're not sure." Dacia looked out the window, wondering if Bryce and Alvin had made it back to campus yet. "Bryce's hand stopped about an inch short of Cody's face. We didn't stick around to see what happened. We took off running and didn't stop until we were under the lights."

Cody folded his hands together and eyed the food. "Can we eat now?"

"Yeah, the food's over here." With a hint of guilt in her voice, Samantha said, "It's been here for about fifteen minutes. I ate some of my fries while I waited for you." She rubbed her arms. "I guess I should've been there trying to save you. I just figured whatever Cody wanted to talk to you about took longer than he expected."

Cody didn't want to think about that. Even after their confrontation with Bryce and Alvin, her response still cut him to the core. He thought for sure that she would say yes. He thought this would be the happiest day of his life. Somehow, he'd let himself believe that she felt the same way about him that he felt about her. Instead, he had to figure out how to live the rest of his life with her as a friend and nothing more. Cody opened up his Styrofoam container. "Don't worry, Sam," he said around a bite of his burger. "You'd've never found us."

By the time they finished eating, it was nearly nine o'clock.

"I should leave before Marcy kicks me out." Cody stood up and walked toward the door. He still had plenty of time, but he needed some space. He needed to go lick his wounds so he could figure things out before he saw Dacia again.

As he reached for the handle, Dacia asked in a small voice, "Will you walk with me to Sarah's office tomorrow?"

He turned around, wondering what had brought this on. "Yeah, why?"

"I better talk to her about what happened tonight."

"Yeah, you should." Cody walked back to the men's dorm. He tucked his hands into his pockets and slumped his shoulders, watching his feet. He shouldn't have let Drew get into his head, and maybe he wouldn't have if Dacia hadn't told him about her lesson today.

It was time for him to realize they would only ever be friends.

Chapter 7

Nightmares

Cody rushed across the parking lot. He hadn't had time to change out of his thin pajama pants, but he had grabbed his Bittersweet Lions hoodie on his way out the door. He'd thrown it on as he ran down the stairs. His hair stuck up at odd angles, and even though Samantha's phone call had pulled him from a deep sleep, he was wide awake now.

Dacia held the door open, and Cody rushed in. He stared at her, trying to figure out what was going on. "Samantha sounded like something awf—" Dacia turned just slightly, and he noticed the rag she held to her face. He clenched his jaw, and a sharp pain tore through it. He slowly lifted his hand and pulled the washcloth off her cheek. "Who did that to you?" His eyes narrowed to thin slits, and his voice rose.

Dacia covered his mouth. "Another nightmare. But, I woke up with this. And my pajama shirt torn to shreds."

"How … how did that happen?" He reached toward her cheek but pulled away before touching it. "It's bleeding." His insides twisted in response to the confusion and pain in her eyes. He hated seeing her hurt.

She pressed the rag to her face. "Good grief."

He followed her up the steps to the third floor. She turned and held her finger over her lips. They were only a few steps from Dacia's room when Marcy stepped into the hallway.

"Cody Hawks! What are you doing here at this time of night?"

He pointed at Dacia. "Dacia fell out of her loft, so Samantha called me to come get her and drive her to the doctor."

Dacia pulled the washrag away so that Marcy could see the cut.

"How did you fall out of your loft?" she asked like she was addressing a two-year-old.

"I went to climb down my ladder and didn't realize my foot was asleep. As soon as I put weight on it, I fell. Those things are dangerous, you know."

"Well, just get out of here before somebody else sees you," Marcy instructed. She strode back into her room and slammed the door behind her.

"Good thinking," Dacia said as she reached for her doorknob. "Maybe I should get a ladder to lower from my window. Then you could climb in without Marcy finding out. Or maybe we could tie some sheets together and throw them down to you."

Sarah and Samantha stood by Dacia's bunk, whispering.

"Let me see your face." Sarah hurried over to Dacia.

"I'm not sure, but I think I'm going to need stitches."

Her words tightened the knot in his gut. He wanted to whisk her away from here, to hide her away from the prophecy, the demon, and whatever else might hurt her.

"What do you think?" Dacia had never been one to obsess over her appearance, but she looked fearful. Stitches on her cheek would leave a nasty scar, and she had to know that.

"Oh, dear." Sarah gasped. "I think we should have you see the school nurse. You might at least need butterfly stitches. We'll have to think of something to tell everyone."

"Marcy jumped us in the hallway." Cody went on to explain their conversation. "Think we should stick to that story."

"Yeah, I know how rumors spread, and it would be best to tell everyone the same thing." Sarah nodded her agreement. "Why don't we take you over to the nurse's office? I'll call her and let her know we're on our way. Then we can come back here, and you can tell us what happened. Is that okay with you, Dacia?"

Dacia walked toward the door and nodded as she stuffed her bare feet into her shoes.

"We're coming, too." Cody looked at Dacia's blood-soaked pillow before jogging the few steps to her side.

"There was no doubt in my mind," Sarah responded.

Sarah led the way to the nurse's office, setting a faster pace than Cody expected. When they arrived, Nancy Heron, the school nurse, was waiting for them. "Come in, come in." Her voice was far too chipper for the circumstances. They weren't there for afternoon tea. They were there because Dacia was injured. The short, heavy-set woman smiled at all of them as they walked inside. Her flowery robe was evidence they'd woken her, too. "This is the second accident I've had this weekend."

"How is Bryce?"

Cody winced when Dacia asked that. She couldn't deny that she knew what happened to him. She might as well have admitted her guilt.

"He'll live," Nurse Heron answered gruffly. "Now, let me have a look at your face."

Dacia pulled the washrag down for the umpteenth time. Her hand trembled slightly. Cody wanted to reach for it, to comfort her, but he kept back. If she needed him, he would be there, but he wasn't going to keep pushing himself on her if that wasn't what she wanted.

"How did this happen, dear?"

"I went to step out of my loft. My foot was asleep, and I fell off the ladder." Dacia winced like she'd taken a big gulp of curdled milk.

Nurse Heron walked Dacia over to the table and motioned for her to sit while she pulled on gloves, grabbed antiseptic, and began cleaning the wound. "What did you cut yourself on?"

"I don't know." Dacia looked at Sarah like she was hoping she answered that correctly.

"It's a clean cut." Nurse Heron held onto her cheek and tilted her head toward the light. "I think we can get by with butterfly stitches. I'll give you some bandages to wear over it for the next couple of days. I'm afraid it will scar. If you're lucky, it will be fairly thin and not too noticeable."

Cody stood between Samantha and Sarah while the nurse tended to Dacia. He watched intently, not blinking. None of this made sense. As far as he knew, nothing like it had happened to Dacia before, so why now?

As soon as Dacia hopped off the table, Sarah said, "Wait outside for me while I talk to Nancy."

They strode to the door without saying anything. Cody kept glancing at Dacia. The bandage covered nearly half of her face, and his stomach churned, not because it looked bad but because he hated to see her hurt.

"What a beautiful night." Dacia's voice broke through his thoughts. When he turned toward her, she waved her hand in an arch. "Look at all of the stars."

A crescent moon hung on a black velvet sky amidst millions of twinkling lights. He stared up and felt a sense of calmness wash over him.

"A fairy!" Dacia shouted.

Cody immediately snapped his head around, looking for the mythical creature. A moth hung in the air in front of Dacia. He stared at it for a second and then saw her for what she really was. The fairy had long, silver hair, wide blue eyes, and silver and blue wings. She screeched something before darting off.

"Did you see it?" Dacia bounced up and down and squealed like a little kid.

"Right before she disappeared." He still couldn't believe it. Did this mean everything existed? Did it mean the prophecy was real? "Holy crap."

Sarah opened the door and walked outside. She looked at each of their faces, then tilted her head to the side. "Why do the three of you look so excited?"

"We saw a fairy!" Samantha clapped her hands together in excitement. "She was beautiful."

Sarah sighed. "It's been a long time since I've seen one. I wish I'd have come outside earlier."

"She wasn't what I expected." Dacia stared in the direction the fairy had flown. "She looked like a moth, not a dragonfly."

"That was just an example." Sarah waved her hand in the air. "Think of fairies like birds. There are so many varieties." She glanced wistfully over her shoulder before walking away. "How did you know it was Bryce?" Sarah released a deep breath. "Do I even want to know?"

Cody summarized their trip to Falcon Lake. His fingers tightened into fists when he got to the point where Alvin had threatened Dacia.

When he finished, Dacia said, "We were going to see you about it in the morning."

Sarah folded her hands together, then released them. "Bryce's hand was badly bruised with four broken bones." Disappointment laced her voice. "Nurse Heron suspected it had been crushed, but he was very evasive when she questioned him."

Dacia's face dropped, and for a moment, Cody thought she might cry. "I only meant to keep him from hitting Cody."

Cody reached over and squeezed her shoulder, hoping that his touch could be some comfort to her. "Maybe they'll back off now."

"No … probably not." She held onto his hand. "Now, I actually deserve their anger."

"Don't blame yourself," Sarah said in a firm voice. "Those boys shouldn't have hidden in the trees waiting to ambush you. Violence begets violence."

"If you wouldn't've stopped him, I'd have two bruised cheeks." Cody rubbed his jaw with his other hand.

Samantha lifted one shoulder to her ear. "Who knows what else would've happened?"

"None of you understand what it's like to do this to somebody." Dacia jerked her hand off of Cody's, glaring at each of them. "If you had punched Bryce, you would've meant to"—she waved her arms through the air while explaining her position—"and you would've known what you were doing to him, how much force you inflicted. Don't get me wrong. I'm glad we got away from them. I'm glad you didn't get hit again. But, Bryce shouldn't have gotten hurt as badly as he did."

Cody shook his head. "What you don't understand, is if he hadn't gotten hurt that bad, he would've been able to catch us. Or, Alvin would've taken off after us. Then you might've gotten hurt."

Dacia stopped abruptly. "I'm the one who should've been hurt!"

"Dacia, Cody knew what he was getting himself into." Samantha sighed. "He can't keep himself from trying to protect you. He cares about you too much."

"She's right." Cody looked down at the ground, kicking at a crack in the sidewalk. Samantha didn't know about the conversation he'd had with Dacia. She didn't know that Dacia admitted she only wanted to be friends, so he couldn't blame her for bringing it up. "I wouldn't let anything bad happen to you if I could prevent it."

"I put him in that position." Sarah turned toward the group of friends. "I'm the one who suggested he start walking to and from your lessons with you. Cody has been following my instructions."

Dacia clutched the hair at the top of her head and stared up at the sky. "Sarah, you had nothing to do with it. I'm the one who stayed at the lake with him until after dark." She took a deep breath, and her next words were a whisper. "I never should've let Cody put himself in that position."

"What?" Cody couldn't believe she'd already forgotten how things had happened. "You wanted to go with Samantha. I made you stay."

They walked back to Samantha's and Dacia's room without another word. Everyone seemed to be lost in their thoughts.

Samantha unlocked the door, and they hustled into the room. Dacia walked straight to the refrigerator and pulled out a bottle of water. "Does anybody else want something to drink?"

Everyone said yes, so Dacia passed them out before she sat down in Cookie Monster and started rehashing her nightmare.

"Cody and I were sitting by Falcon Lake. He had his arm around my shoulders, and I was leaning against him." She took a sip of her water, not meeting anyone's gaze before starting again. "The sun was setting, and we were the only ones there, just enjoying the view and the silence. All of a sudden, the wind picked up. I shivered, and he pulled me closer, rubbing my arm."

Cody remembered the feeling of holding her while watching the sunset. He'd wanted her to feel the same way. He'd wanted it so bad that it hurt. *Friendship's good.* Her words replayed over and over again like a record skipping. He closed his eyes, hoping nobody would notice his agony. As soon as he felt in control, he opened them again.

"An eerie feeling crawled along my spine. Something told me to run." She gripped the armrests, and her gaze kept darting toward the door like she wanted to flee. "I tried to shake it off, but the feeling just got more intense. I tried to get Cody up, but he seemed frozen in place. I couldn't even get his arm to budge."

Had he been the reason for her nightmare? Had he been the reason she'd gotten hurt? He shook his head. He didn't want to get lost in his thoughts. He needed to hear what she said.

"A wave crashed against the shore, drawing my attention. Yellow, glowing eyes stared at me from beneath the water." Her words were rushed.

Cody wanted to comfort her, but what if he was the problem? He didn't want to make things worse for her.

"I struggled to pull myself out from under Cody's arm. I dug my feet into the ground, trying to get my body free.

"A low voice growled, 'Dacia, give up. You can't win.' A clawed hand the size of my body reached out of the water." She tugged her hand through her hair. "I kicked harder but couldn't free myself. Cody moved, and relief surged through me. I turned toward him, intent on making him leave, but instead of Cody, I peered into Bryce's pale green eyes."

She took another drink. "His hand was wrapped up in bloody bandages, and he told me to look at what I'd done to him." Tears filled her eyes, but they didn't fall. "His fingers were all mangled, and he threatened to get even with me."

Cody felt his gut clench. He didn't doubt that they would try to get even with Dacia, and he hoped he was there to protect her when it happened. Not that she would need him or necessarily want him there.

"I struggled to get away, but Bryce pushed me toward the lake. The icy water crashed against my legs, and my feet slipped out from under me. As soon as I fell into the water, Nefarious grabbed me. His claws dug into me, pinning my arms to my sides. I fought to get free, but I … I was no match for him. I tried to take a deep breath before I went under, but he pulled me down, and water filled my lungs. My chest burned. I knew I was going to drown. My head spun, and I thrashed about, trying to free myself. Then everything went dark."

"So, how did you get the cut on your face?" Samantha's nose was scrunched up in confusion.

"There's more," Dacia said in a robotic voice. She blew a breath out through her mouth before continuing. "I felt myself being pulled out of the water. The light blinded me when I neared the surface, and I couldn't see who was lifting me.

"Nefarious snatched at me, and his claws tore through my shirt. I jerked around and realized that nobody was helping me." She rubbed her hands over the arms of the chair, forward and backward, then forward again. "I was flying above the lake. Nefarious looked up at me through the water. His yellow eyes were all that I could make out."

Her posture was rigid, and the words came out much faster than she normally talked. "Ice shot from my hands, and in a matter of seconds, Falcon Lake froze solid."

Frost spread from beneath Dacia's hands. Crystals formed, branching out as they covered every inch of Cookie Monster. The blue, fuzzy chair turned into a giant ice cube in a matter of seconds. He couldn't tear his eyes away. It was like watching a time-lapse scene in a nature documentary. He'd seen her do all sorts of things but never anything like this. How did she not realize it? Wasn't she freezing?

Samantha covered her mouth with her hand and pointed.

"What?" Dacia snapped.

Sarah kept her voice calm like she was speaking to a scared or injured animal. "Dacia, why don't you try to calm down?"

"I'm fine," she forced out through clenched teeth. "Just stop looking at me like that!"

"It's, uh, hard to." Cody rubbed his hand over his face, hoping to stop stumbling over his words. "You're sitting on a froz—a frozen chair."

Samantha nodded but didn't say anything.

"Wha …" Dacia threw her arms up and jumped out of the chair.

"It's okay, Dacia." Sarah lifted her hands and slowly bobbed them up and down.

Dacia dragged her fingers through her hair, and a nervous laugh tumbled out of her. "I guess that's why I felt so cold all of a sudden."

While Dacia stood in front of the chair, the ice receded. Once it was gone, the fabric wasn't even wet. She bent over with her hands on her knees. "I have to get a grip on my powers. This is getting ridiculous."

Friendship's good. Her words rang through his mind like a warning bell, but he couldn't stand to see her so upset. He got up and slowly made his way over to her. He rubbed her shoulder, and when she didn't pull away, he bent down so that his mouth was right next to her ear. His words were only for her. "You're okay. You don't have to talk to us anymore."

She squeezed his hand. "I'll finish." She sat on the edge of the chair, and Cody stood sentinel beside her. "I hovered above the lake. A noise came from beneath the surface, growing louder until the lake exploded. Shards of ice flew through the air. I tried to dodge them all, but one sliced through my cheek. Nefarious rose out of the water. His body was covered in bright red flames. He threw his head back and roared.

"The nightmare was vivid and terrifying." Her hands trembled, and she folded them together in her lap. "But waking up wounded … what am I supposed to think of that?"

What do I to say to that? Cody wondered, but he couldn't think of a single thing.

Samantha must have felt the same way. She stood with her arms folded over her chest and stared at the ground.

Sarah shook her head. "My grandfather never warned me about anything like this."

"I don't know if I'll be able to get any more sleep tonight—" Dacia covered a yawn "—but you should try."

"Yes, you're right." Sarah stood. "You need to try to sleep, too."

"I'm a little scared to close my eyes." Dacia stared at the wall instead of any of them. "What if next time, it's more than just a cut?"

Sarah walked a couple of steps toward her and squeezed her shoulder. "I don't know what to tell you."

"Before you go, you should see this." Samantha held up Dacia's pajama shirt.

Sarah looked from the ruined top to Dacia, and Cody wrapped his arm around her shoulders. "You're going to be all right."

"I hope you're right, Cody." Dacia slumped against his side.

Sarah ran her fingers along the slashes. "I assume that happened when Nefarious grabbed you."

"That's my guess." Dacia lifted a shoulder but stayed against Cody's side.

Sarah pinched the bridge of her nose. "I'm going to have to think about this." She turned to Cody. "Come on. Let's get out of here so these two can get some rest. It would be best if I went with you. That way Marcy won't be able to say anything."

Chapter 8

Her Knight In Faded Denim

Cody sat in Geography, watching the clock instead of listening to Dr. Cedar. The teacher leaned against the edge of his desk with his arms resting on the top of his stomach. His gaze darted around the class, stopping frequently on Cody's face.

Cody tried to give the man his attention. He was a good teacher and a genuinely good guy, but Cody couldn't concentrate. He'd left too late and missed walking Dacia to her class.

Samantha had looked a little shaken when she opened the door, so he'd asked what was going on.

"Dacia's cut is gone." She'd held onto her pendant and slid it back and forth over the fine, gold chain. "I don't get it."

He'd stood there, staring at her for way too long, trying to figure out what she was saying. How could Dacia's wound have healed already? As he turned to walk away, he decided that maybe it wasn't that strange. It never should have happened in the first place.

Cody had tried to catch up to Dacia, but she was already sitting in Speech.

Dr. Cedar dismissed class, and Cody grabbed his bag, slinging it over his shoulder. He jogged down the stairs, squeezing between students.

"Cody." Dr. Cedar's voice was a sharp command that Cody dared not ignore.

Cody's shoulders slumped at the sound of it. He didn't usually leave after class because his next one was in the same room. He walked toward the desk, trying not to look too put out. "What's up?"

"Everything okay?" Dr. Cedar's friendly eyes filled with concern. "You didn't take notes, and you don't usually leave."

Cody glanced at the clock. "Worried 'bout a friend. Need to check on her." He resituated his backpack on his shoulder. "Might be late."

"Well, go on then." He patted Cody's upper arm. "Get out of here."

Cody ran out the front door of Primrose Hall. He looked at Quartz Building when he sprinted by, wondering if he should check inside, but he doubted that Dacia was still in there.

"Yo, Cody," Justin hollered as he went by.

Cody lifted his hand into the air and kept going. He needed to see Dacia. He needed to know how she was holding up.

He jogged, searching the mass exodus of students, hoping to see her face. He skipped by the large groups, knowing she wouldn't be in one of them by choice. Then he noticed someone walking alone. Her red hair bounced against her shoulders. As he neared her, she sped up, but he was still gaining. He was almost to her when she stopped and spun around. She lifted her hands in front of her like she was ready to defend herself.

Her jaw dropped, and she shook her head. "Cody Hawks, don't you ever do that again!" She lowered her hands. "I figured you were one of them. You're lucky I didn't hurt you!"

"Sorry." He walked toward her, lifting his palms so they faced out, a sign of surrender. "Needed to see if you were okay."

She looked anywhere but at him. "Did you see Samantha? Did she tell you about my face?"

"Yeah." He touched the bandage. "I don't get it."

"Me either." She pulled away from him, and his heart clenched.

Friendship's good. Not wanting to crowd her or make her uncomfortable, he took a step back.

She finally looked up at him. "Aren't you supposed to be in class?"

Did she not want him here? Would things be uncomfortable between them from now on? Had he screwed everything up? He looked down and kicked the dirt. "Was worried. You had class with your archenemies. Wanted to make sure you were safe."

"So, now they're my archenemies, are they?" She bumped her hip into him, and his head snapped up.

Was she okay with him being around?

Smiling at him, she said, "I always wanted to be a comic book superhero."

Cody laughed.

"It's very sweet of you, but you can't keep skipping your classes."

"Who says I'm skipping?" He jerked his head back and pointed at himself. "I'm fashionably late. There's a difference."

"You'd better get going." She pressed on his chest, nudging him away. "I guess I'm going to go back. I'll just sit in the classroom and work on my speech assignment." She turned around and started walking back the way they'd come from.

"You should work on your book report instead." He tilted his head to the side, wondering if she had somehow finished it or if the speech was actually due first. "Although, you could buy the food for a change."

"Oh, didn't I tell you?" She shot him a crooked grin that made his heart skip a beat or two. "I got up early this morning and put the final touches on it, so I guess you're buying. Samantha's counting on it."

"I shouldn't bet against you." She was a drug that he couldn't get enough of. He shouldn't want to spend time with her. It would be better for him to stay away from her as much as possible, but even though he knew that, he was looking forward to seeing her Friday, to buying her pizza. "It gives you the kick-in-the-butt you need." He held the door to Quartz Building open for her, wondering if he should walk her to her classroom or leave her here. Her hand brushed against his as she walked inside, sending the kaleidoscope of butterflies inside him into a frenzy, and that made up his mind. "You can go alone from here. Be a good girl, and don't leave."

Cody walked back to Dr. Cedar's classroom in Primrose Hall. He was late, but knowing that Dacia was okay, it would be easier to concentrate. She was next door, and he would see her again in less than an hour.

Dr. Cedar nodded at Cody when he took his seat. Cody gave him a thumbs-up, and Dr. Cedar smiled. Throughout class, Cody took notes and answered questions, but as soon as it was over, he was ready to leave. The Potato Heads were in English Lit with Dacia and him next period, and he wanted to get there before them.

He didn't make it. His feet faltered when he stepped through the doorway. He sucked in a deep breath and hurried to Dacia's side. "They bother you?"

"No, I don't think Bryce will be a problem until his hand heals." She looked at them through the corner of her eyes. "Alvin could be an issue if I run into him by myself. He seems to be holding a grudge." She rubbed her arm and chewed on her bottom lip. "Hopefully, I won't have to worry about it, though. I don't want to hurt anybody else."

Cody knocked on Dacia's door fifteen minutes before she and Samantha had to leave for Advanced Algebra. "Your escort has arrived," he said, holding out his arm for Dacia to take. "You ready, Samantha?"

"Yeah." She grabbed her backpack, and the three of them took off.

Alvin and Vanessa stood outside Kalmia Hall. "So, now, you can't go anywhere without Cody." Alvin's lip curled into a snarl.

Cody stepped forward, but Dacia put her hand on his chest, stopping him. "I don't recall either of you walking alone."

"It doesn't matter. We can wait." Vanessa's face twisted with anger. They turned and walked into the building, slamming the door behind them.

"Wait? For what?" Samantha fiddled with the strap of her backpack.

"Don't know." Cody turned toward Dacia. Fear for her tightened his stomach. "Don't go anywhere without me."

"I know. I know." She threw the door open and stomped inside.

Cody followed her through the crowded hallway and into the classroom. He sat next to her, situating himself in a way that he hoped blocked her view of Alvin and Vanessa.

About halfway through class, she leaned over and whispered, "He's going to try to get even with me. Why can't he just realize the same thing will happen to him?"

Cody set his hand on top of hers but said nothing. When class ended, he watched Alvin and Vanessa leave, waiting a few seconds longer before gathering his things.

"Alvin was making me nervous in there," Samantha said when they stepped outside. "He kept shooting daggers at you."

"Noticed that." Cody clenched and unclenched his fists. The action did little to calm him. "Don't even open your door without me around."

"Cody"—Dacia stopped walking and put her hands on her hips—"I appreciate your concern, but I can't spend my life hiding from the Potato Heads."

"Know you can handle yourself. But I …" He rubbed the back of his neck. "I worry about you, and I'd never forgive myself if something happened to you, especially if I could've prevented it."

Dacia's stance relaxed a little. "Thanks, but sometimes I'm going to be by myself. You can't keep that from happening, and chances are that if Alvin tries to attack me, he'll end up wishing we'd never met."

He knew she was right. He knew that, after having his hand crushed, Bryce probably felt that way. He also knew he would worry if he wasn't with her. He had always felt the need to protect her, and that wasn't going to change just because she only wanted to be friends.

After lunch, Cody pressed his hand to the small of Dacia's back, keeping her pace even with his. His gaze darted from side to side. Alvin and Vanessa had made it clear that they were going to get even with Dacia, and he would do everything in his power to keep that from happening. Dacia had called him her knight in faded denim, and he had every intention of protecting her as a knight would his queen.

"Hello," Sarah said when they stepped into her office.

Cody stood with his hands on his hips, blocking the door. "Under no circumstances is Dacia to leave here on her own."

"Why?" Sarah looked from him to Dacia then back again. "What happened?"

"Alvin and Vanessa seem to be trying to figure out how to get even with me." Dacia rolled her eyes.

Cody shook his head, not understanding how she wasn't taking this seriously.

"They were waiting for me to show up to algebra and weren't very happy to see that I had an escort." Using her thumb, she pointed over her shoulder at Cody.

"Oh." Sarah shook her head. "I'll have a talk with them. I'll tell them to quit harassing you."

Dacia ran her fingers through her hair. "I'd rather you didn't. They hate me enough as it is. I don't need them thinking I'm a tattletale too."

"While I can understand that," Sarah said, "I have to do something, and it'd be best if you didn't go out alone."

A sense of satisfaction washed over Cody when she said that. He nodded his agreement. "I'll walk with her."

"I'll be lucky to go to the bathroom by myself," Dacia muttered.

Sarah rubbed her chin. "What was that, Dacia?"

"Oh, I'm lucky somebody wants to watch out for me."

"Yes, you are." Her head bobbed up and down. "Cody, why don't you come back in about two hours?"

"Sounds good." He waved on his way out the door and pulled his phone out of his pocket. He set a timer on it to be sure he was back to pick up Dacia on time. He didn't want to give her any excuse to leave without him, although having Sarah on his side made him relax slightly. He didn't think Dacia would fight her on this one.

Without really thinking about it, he made his way to the court.

"Yo, Cody," Drew hollered at him from inside the fence. "Join in. We need another guy. Bryce is out for a while."

Cody quickly assessed the teams and realized he would be skins. He pulled his shirt off as he walked through the gate and tossed it to the side. His teammates came up and bumped fists with him. Then he threw the ball in to Justin.

Cody jogged down the court and took his position at guard. Tyler moved into his defensive stance, stretching his hand out, nearly touching Cody's chest. "Heard you were there. What happened?" He glanced up into Cody's eyes for just a moment before looking back at the ball.

"Bryce punched me." Cody turned his face so Tyler could see the greenish-colored bruise. "Then got what he deserved."

Drew looked across the key at him. "Dude, you broke his hand."

"Nope." Cody caught the ball, squared up, and sunk his shot. Jogging down the court, he said, "Didn't lay a hand on him. Had Dacia with me. Didn't want her hurt." He planted himself between Tyler and the basket, then rubbed his jaw. "Owe him one when he heals, though."

Nobody brought up Bryce for the rest of the game, and Cody was grateful for that. Until the other night, Cody had never had an issue with him. Now, hearing Bryce's name made rage flare through him like a wildfire in strong winds.

When Cody's timer went off, he bowed out of the game. "Thanks for the game. Got somewhere I need to be." He picked up his shirt and pulled it on as he jogged to Cacomistle Hall.

As Cody walked into Sarah's office, Sarah looked from the doorway to Dacia. Her brow was furrowed, and it was obvious that she was perplexed. "How did you know that?"

"Uh … I don't know." Dacia sounded just as confused as Sarah looked. "I just sensed it."

Cody walked up to the couch where Dacia was sitting and asked, "What'd you sense?"

"Dacia informed me moments before your arrival that you were here. I just wondered how she knew," Sarah explained.

Without a hint of surprise in his voice, he said, "Stranger things've happened." Two nights ago, she had frozen her chair while sitting in it. Sensing that he had arrived didn't seem like much compared to that. He turned to Dacia. "You ready, or you need longer?"

"I'm ready." Dacia stood up, grabbing her bag off the floor as she did. "I'll see you later, Sarah."

"Let me know if anything comes up." Sarah pinned Dacia with a stern look.

"I will."

When they were on the sidewalk, Cody asked, "How'd things go?"

"You know, they went pretty well." Dacia smiled up at him and, at the same time, puffed her chest out.

He relaxed a little. This was the first time in a long time that he could remember her looking like she was proud of herself.

"Sarah had me try to intentionally use my powers." She watched a bird fly out of one of the pine trees surrounding the sidewalk. It landed in front of them in the grass, hopping further away with each step they took. "I froze a bowl full of water." Her voice rose with each word.

Cody nodded. He wanted to throw his arm over her shoulders and pull her against his side, but besides being sweaty from playing basketball, he also didn't want to overstep the friendship boundary. "Cool. Not surprised."

"I know you're not." She wrapped her hand around his bicep. "I think I'm beginning to gain some of that confidence in myself. Maybe if I can keep accidents from happening it will eventually grow into a full-blown case of self-esteem."

Cody wanted to drag out the walk back to the girls' dorm, but night was closing in quickly. It was twilight when they left Sarah's office, and if Alvin wanted to ambush them again, it would be easy enough in the dying light.

So instead of strolling along with Dacia, enjoying the evening, he put his hand on the small of her back, forcing her to hustle to keep up with his long strides. He kept an eye out for anything out of the ordinary and cocked his head to the side, listening for any unusual sounds.

"You know, Cody, maybe a confrontation would be good."

"What do you mean?" Cody stopped under the glow of one of the streetlights. "Are you nuts? I'm trying to protect you, and you want to battle it out." He shook his head, waiting for her to explain.

She cleared her throat, and determination flared in her green eyes. "Until we do, we are going to be on edge, waiting for somebody to jump out of the bushes. The only way they are going to leave us alone is if I do the same type of thing to them that I did to Bryce." Her face slackened, dropping her bottom jaw slightly. "If I could get a few minutes alone with Bryce or

Cassandra, maybe they could convince the others to back off. Maybe they'd realize that nothing good can come from this."

"Don't know, but it's better than confronting them." They started walking toward the dorms again. After a few steps, Cody said, "Do you remember … Oh, never mind."

"What? You can ask me whatever it is."

He dropped his chin, wanting his words to only be for her, but not wanting to lose sight of his surroundings. His voice was unsteady. "Remember saying Nefarious can control humans?"

"Yes, I do, and yes, I think it's safe to assume he's the puppet master in charge of them." She inhaled a deep breath, then slowly released it. "Thinking that is what leads me to believe I may need to hurt them in order to get them out from under his thumb."

Not caring anymore, he draped his arm over her shoulders. Somehow, he needed to figure out how to protect her. They walked the rest of the way to the dorm like that. Cody told himself multiple times that he needed to let go of her, but his arm wouldn't follow through with the command. No matter how many times he thought it, the other voice in his head reminded him that Dacia hadn't pulled away.

Chapter 9

Beaten And Broken

Cody cut across the parking lot between the dorms. He knew Dacia was concerned about talking to Bryce and Cassandra, so he wasn't sure if the gray and dismal dawn was because of her or if it was the natural weather.

Early in the morning, there were only a few other students out and about in this area. He stepped over the curb onto the grass between the parking lot and the narrow, seldom-used sidewalk.

A noise in the bushes startled him. He stopped and watched Bryce and Cassandra step out from behind them. Bryce held up his injured hand, showing Cody the cast. "What kind of a freak is your girlfriend anyway?"

"What girlfriend?" Cody smirked even though Bryce's insult burned his insides.

Cassandra's gaze darted to something behind him. He started to turn, but a bat smashed into his knee, knocking him to the ground.

He shouted as he fell. Pressing his hands down on the ground, he pushed himself up, but Alvin swung at his knee again. Something snapped, and a pained moan slipped through Cody's clenched teeth.

Bryce knelt in front of Cody and punched him in the mouth, stopping him from crying out again. Then they all joined in. Kicking. Punching. Pummeling him with the bat. He heard his ribs crack. His eyes swelled, making it nearly impossible to see.

"Enough," Bryce said, and the battering stopped. "Pick him up."

Alvin got behind Cody and hoisted him none too gently, holding him in front of Bryce. "This is for my hand." He threw two punches at Cody's face and then two to his ribs.

They threw him behind the bushes. Branches poked and scraped him, but he could hardly feel anything through the throbbing. He landed with his leg twisted behind him.

"Your girlfriend's next." Cody's head pounded, making it impossible to tell who said it. Their laughter grew quieter as they walked off.

He tried to push himself to his feet. He needed to get to Dacia, to warn her that they were coming for her, but he couldn't move. With every breath, pain tore through his chest.

Each of his wounds pulsed, and he could feel the injuries swelling. But the worst of it was the words echoing in his mind. *Your girlfriend's next.* He wrapped his arm around his aching ribs. *Your girlfriend's next.* His heartbeat pounded in his ears. The sound was deafening, but it still couldn't drown out the voice. *Your girlfriend's next.*

He'd failed her. He was supposed to be able to keep her safe, but he couldn't even defend himself. He hadn't even gotten in a single hit. She needed someone better than him. Someone stronger. Someone who could give more than they got in a fight.

That obviously wasn't him.

He was a failure.

Knowing that whatever they did to her was because of his ineptitude, how could she ever look at him again?

The adrenaline fled from his body, and he lay behind the bushes, trembling.

Black clouds blocked out the sun's light. Lightning flashed, only to be immediately answered by the crash of thunder.

This storm had to be of Dacia's making. He pictured her as broken as he felt, her beautiful face battered and bleeding.

He should have been there for her. He should have been better.

"Hey, Cody," Dacia's voice shook, and he wondered how badly they had hurt her.

He tried to peel his eyes open, but they wouldn't part.

"I'm here. I'm going to help you." She ran her fingers through his hair.

He fought to keep from grimacing. Every inch of his body hurt. Every touch was like razors slicing his skin.

"Do you think you can lean on me and try walking?"

He moved his head down to his chest ever so slowly. Pain racked his body, but he tried to keep her from seeing it.

Fat raindrops fell from the sky. Each one that touched his skin felt like a hot iron branding him.

Somehow, she pulled him to his feet. Cody bit back a yelp and settled all his weight on one leg. He heard the rain falling behind them as Dacia led him presumably to the nurse's office. He figured he must have been hurt worse than he originally thought because he could feel his arm draped over her shoulders. Each hair that fell over the top of it stung his hypersensitive skin. He felt her hand holding his, and her other arm wrapped around his waist, but he couldn't feel his feet hitting the ground. His weight should've dragged her down, but they kept moving.

His body ached. The effort of holding his head up was too much for him. His chin dropped to his chest. His shoulders hunched. Even though he was slumped forward, she kept going.

A door opened at the same time that the storm let loose. Rain splashed up on his legs. He could feel that, so why couldn't he feel himself walking?

"Oh, my!" Nurse Heron said. "What happened to him?"

Cody tried to answer but only winced in pain.

"I left my dorm and found him this way." Dacia was breaking. He could hear it in her voice. "Can I use your phone to call Sa—uh, Dean Aspen?"

"Yes, dear, it's over there," Nurse Heron answered. "Help me get him back here first, though."

His arm was lifted over the nurse's shoulder, and suddenly, he could feel his foot on the ground and every staggering, agonizing step after that. They helped him sit on the table, then carefully lifted his legs onto it. He stifled a shout, relaxing a little when it was over.

"I'll be right back," Dacia whispered in Cody's ear.

He grabbed her fingers and squeezed.

While she was gone, the nurse took his blood pressure, listened to his heart and lungs, poked and prodded him, and cleaned his wounds. Each time she touched him, he wanted to scream, but he held it in, afraid Dacia might hear.

He knew her. He knew she would blame herself for this, and he didn't want to make it any worse.

"This is going to be cold," Nurse Heron said before placing an icepack over his eyes.

The door opened. The click of heels against the tiles let Cody know it wasn't Dacia.

"Cody. Nancy."

Sarah's voice shouldn't have surprised him, but it did.

"The ambulance is on the way," Nancy said without preamble. "It should be here in fifteen minutes or so. I cleaned his wounds and gave him fentanyl. If the paramedics need to, they can give it to him again."

For the next few minutes, they talked too quietly for Cody to make out what they were saying. The door opened and closed, then opened again. Soft footsteps padded over to the bed, and he would have recognized them anywhere.

Dacia placed her hand on top of his.

"Dacia—" Cody struggled to talk "—thanks."

"Yeah," she said, then paused for a few seconds. "I just wish I could've stopped this from happening."

"You need to—" Agony brought Cody's words to a halt. He focused on his breathing, hoping the pain would diminish.

Dacia squeezed his hand. "Don't talk."

"Calm down … stop rain." He wished he could look up at her, reassure her that he would be fine.

"Yeah." There was a long pause, and Cody pictured her dragging her hand through her hair. "It'd make it easier for the ambulance."

"Want you—" he winced "—come hospital with me."

"I'll follow the ambulance. I won't let you go alone."

"No, with me." Moving his mouth was torture, but he had to get it out before the drugs made it too hard to think. "Need you."

"I will if they'll let me, Cody, but I can't promise anything." She twined her fingers through his and rubbed his hand with her thumb. It was about the only part of his body that didn't ache. "Why don't you try to save your energy now? I'll stay right here with you."

He listened to their breathing, hers steady, his much harsher, and the sound of the rain. It slowed from the deluge that it had been but didn't stop.

A door slammed outside, and soon after, Nurse Heron came back into the room. There were other people with her, but Cody couldn't tell how many.

"Ma'am, we'll need you to move," a guy said. His tone was all business.

Dacia's voice shook slightly when she said, "Cody wants me to ride along with him."

"Are you related?" the man asked while checking Cody's pulse.

"Yes, I'm his sister."

"As soon as we get him loaded, you can climb in the ambulance," a new voice responded. "Okay, Cody." There was a pause while Cody assumed somebody verified that was his name. "We're going to move you now. We're going to go easy, but it'll probably hurt."

Cody tried to suck in a deep breath to prepare, but sharp, excruciating pains shot through his chest.

While he was still trying to get a handle on his agony, they lifted him onto a stretcher.

Pain tore through his body. Piercing, throbbing, burning anguish that he thought would never end. The sound that was ripped from his lungs was inhuman.

They rolled the stretcher through the door out into the drizzling rain and hefted Cody into the ambulance. Then the second EMT said, "Come on, Little Sister."

Knowing she would be with him eased Cody's mind. Dacia climbed in and took his hand in hers.

The first EMT started asking questions as soon as the ambulance took off, but Cody was too drowsy to answer any of them. The words blended into something completely unrecognizable.

Chapter 10

Recovery

Cody didn't remember anything that happened after leaving campus. He woke up in a hospital room, listening to what he assumed was the steady beeping of a heart monitor.

A slight squeaking of the hinges alerted him to the door opening. He didn't bother turning. He couldn't see anything. Besides, he figured it was a nurse. As the footsteps neared, he realized it was Dacia.

The bed sank down next to him, and her hand covered his. "How are you doing, Cody?"

"Sore," he whispered. "Glad you're here." His jaw ached.

"Samantha and Sarah are here, too," she said.

"Hey." The word rolled out of his mouth on a moan. "Gave me pain pills, so I'll fall asleep. Sorry."

"Don't worry, Cody. You need your rest so you can get better." He could barely make out Samantha's voice over the beeping of all the machines.

He tried to stay awake. He wanted to hear what they had to say, but under the influence of the medication, he drifted off quickly.

Something touched his skin, waking him. "Wow, that's cold." He looked at the dark-haired nurse standing above him, holding a stethoscope to his chest.

"Sorry about that," Tammy, according to her nametag, said. "I didn't mean to wake you, but I have to take your vitals."

"It's okay." He looked around the room and found Dacia watching him from a chair next to his bed. "Where are Samantha and Sarah?"

Tammy finished what she was doing and left.

"They went to get lunch." Dacia scooted the chair a little closer. "You can open your eyes! And you sound a lot better."

"Yeah, feel better." He tried to push himself into a more comfortable position, but pain ripped through him. He collapsed onto the bed, hoping she couldn't see how badly he hurt. "Must be a wonder drug. Good to see you, though."

Crimson stained her cheeks. "I'm glad you're better, but you still have quite a way to go." She turned away from him and wiped the tears off of her face.

"What's wrong?" He reached up and brushed away the ones she missed, letting his hand linger. "Why you crying?"

She closed her eyes and pressed against his palm. "I'm worried about you. You looked really bad for a while."

"Yeah, I'm sure." He pulled his hand away, remembering that he had failed her, remembering that she needed someone stronger. "Won't be able to take care of you while I'm on crutches."

"You shouldn't worry—"

Every movement hurt, but he rearranged his expression into something softer, hoping to erase the pain from it. "I always worry about you. Somebody needs to."

"Not now you don't. Just rest, take care of yourself, and get better." She turned away from his face.

His gaze followed hers, and his heart sank when he realized she was looking at his knee. He didn't want her to know how badly it broke him. He would never play basketball again, maybe never even walk right. Nodding at his knee, he said, "It'll be fine. If it's not, I'll deal." He twined his fingers with hers. "Glad you're okay. Didn't know if you'd be. Told me you were next."

"It should—" Dacia cut her words off when the door opened, bringing with it the smell of lunch.

"You look great!" Sarah and Samantha said in unison when they walked in and saw Cody's face.

Cody looked up at Dacia. He knew what she had been about to say, and they would finish this conversation later. When they were alone again, he would set her straight.

"Yeah, I know." His smile didn't feel sincere. He was trying too hard. "Maybe I should be a model."

"Dr. Sequoia told me he could only give you painkillers." Sarah stared at him until he felt like a specimen under a microscope. "I guess he must've decided to give you something else."

"No, that's all they have him on." Dacia moved onto Cody's bed so they could sit.

Maybe it was the painkillers. Maybe Cody just couldn't help himself, but he set his hand on her thigh, grateful that she was by his side.

Dacia smiled down at him, and it seemed sincere. "The nurse was just in here. Before Cody woke up, she said, 'Nobody heals this fast, even when they are on medicine.'"

Cody looked from Dacia to the bags in Sarah's hands. The smell wafting out of them wiped out the sterile scent of the room, and his stomach growled loudly in response. He watched Sarah hand a sack to Dacia and shot her the best puppy-dog eyes that he could muster in his current condition.

"You can have some if you think you can eat it." She held her bag out to him. "I'm sure you can handle the fries at least. You can try some chicken, too, if you'd like."

He grabbed a few of her French fries, wondering how bad it would hurt his jaw to chew them. Earlier, he hadn't been able to talk without nearly unbearable agony, but now, it felt like his injuries were almost a memory. Could the medication take all the pain away? Would it return with a vengeance as the drugs wore off?

He shoved his mouth full and chewed gently at first. When he realized it didn't hurt, he ate at least half of Dacia's lunch.

Dacia reached into her bag, and finding it empty, she got up and threw it in the trash. When she sat back down, she asked, "So how did they do this to you?" She froze for a second, and her eyes widened. Her next words were rushed. "You don't have to tell me now if you don't want to."

Closing his eyes, he let out a long sigh. Their attack flashed through his mind. He hadn't even thrown a punch. He was pathetic. "Hid in the bushes." He stared out the window. He didn't want to talk about it. He didn't want her to know how easy it had been for them.

He clenched his hands, resting them in his lap. His eyes focused somewhere outside while he told them about the attack. After recounting how they said they were going after Dacia next, he looked up at her, hoping she would understand. He had tried to get up. He had wanted nothing more than to warn her, to protect her. Grabbing her hand, he said, "I tried, but guess I'm not your knight in shining armor after all."

"You still are, Cody, but it was my turn to rescue you." There was something hard in her voice, and Cody looked away.

He felt nauseous. His cheeks burned as he pulled his hand out of hers. She had every right to be disgusted by him. Some protector he'd turned out to be.

Ominous storm clouds rolled in, making the room as dark as night.

"Dacia needs a minute," Sarah said.

Cody shook himself out of his stupor and rubbed her arm. This was all his fault. If he could have been stronger, she would be able to control her emotions. He should have been there for her.

The storm clouds weakened as Dacia relaxed.

Sitting on the bed next to him, she looked so much smaller than him, fragile even, compared to his bulk. "Glad you found me." He fought to keep his voice soothing. "How'd you carry me?"

"I, uh … didn't exactly … carry you. You sort of floated along beside me. I guess I can levitate things now, too."

"Thanks." It finally made sense to him why he hadn't felt pain flare up with every step he took. He squeezed her hand. "So … what's going to happen?"

Sarah told Cody about contacting the board members. "The meeting will be later this week or early next week, as soon as everyone can meet."

Cody's eyes darkened, and he nodded.

"I've tried to get in touch with your parents. Nobody was home, so I called their work numbers. Your mom was in a meeting, and your dad is out of town on a business trip." Sarah stood up and put her hand on his shoulder. "Give them a call."

"I will."

"Well, kids"—she grabbed her purse—"I've got to get back to the school. Samantha, would you like to ride with me, then bring Dacia's truck down here, or how would you guys like to handle this?"

"That'd be fine," Samantha said. "Are your keys in our room still?"

"They're in my purse." Dacia nodded. "Will you bring that back with you, too?"

"Sure thing—I'll be back in a bit."

"Take care of yourself, Cody," Sarah said. "I can come back tomorrow morning to see how you're doing and to talk to Dr. Sequoia if you'd like."

He hated the idea of pulling her away. She had more important things to worry about, like making sure Dacia was trained. He tried to shrug, but the tiny movement made his ribs scream in protest. "We'll see how it goes."

Sarah turned to Dacia and a knowing look crossed her face. "Don't stay too late, Dacia. You need your rest, too."

Cody watched, waiting for the door to shut. As soon as it did, he turned to Dacia and said, "Earlier you were gonna say you should be lying here instead of me, but, Dacia, you're wrong."

"No, it shouldn't be you." She shook her head. "Bryce and Cassandra were injured because of me. You were an innocent bystander in all of it. If you hadn't been with me when Bryce jumped me, you wouldn't be here now."

"I'm not an innocent bystander!" Pain tore through him, and he winced. He needed to take it easy. He needed to heal so he could try to protect her. He would do better next time. He wouldn't take shortcuts. He would stick to the busier sidewalks. He would be there when she needed him. If … if she needed him. "I put myself into this position because I can't bear to see you go through this alone. We've been friends for too long."

She grabbed his hand, not acknowledging what he'd said at all. "Calm down, please."

They sat in silence for a while. Dacia stared down at his face for a few minutes before releasing his hand.

"Thanks for riding with me and staying all day." He had so much more he wanted to say, but he didn't want to hurt himself worse, and he didn't want to rile her up again. The storm clouds had begun to clear up, and sunlight filtered in through the windows. "Know it's not fun."

"You'd do the same for me." She looked away from him. "I had to tell them I was your sister to ride along on the ambulance. Then when we got here, one of the paramedics told me that you, my boyfriend, were going to be okay. He said there was no way we were siblings."

"Oh, well, uh—while I was lying behind the bushes, I was thinking about that." He twined his fingers through hers. "I was, uh, I was thinking that … well, that, uh—" he cleared his throat and took a deep breath "—life's short. Maybe we should, uh, go ahead and get together if, uh, you want to."

What the hell? He mentally slapped himself. He'd decided she would be better off without him. Why was he doing this? It had to be the medicine. It had to be affecting his brain. She would just turn him down again, and this time he would lose her. Forever.

When she didn't respond, he knew he had messed things up. Would he be able to fix them? "Dacia?" His voice was small. His heart raced. She was taking forever to answer. What was she thinking?

"Yeah." She squeezed his hand. "Maybe we should."

He sat there for too long, letting the words run through his mind again and again. Had she really said what he thought she said? Did she really want him? Even after he'd failed her?

She gazed down at him. Her green eyes seemed illuminated by an inner light. He could see her excitement burning in them.

He raised his bed to a sitting position, reached his hand over, caressed her cheek, and said, "You really are a sight for sore eyes." Giving her a chance to pull away, he slowly brought his mouth to hers. Their lips touched, and a thousand rockets burst inside of him. He'd wanted this for so long. Their mouths melded together, moving in sync, like they were meant for this.

His hands spread over her back, pulling her closer. A twinge of pain shot through his ribs, but he ignored it. This was worth it.

He was kissing her.

Finally.

When the pain got to be too much, Cody reluctantly pulled away. He lowered his bed, leaned his head back, and closed his eyes to rest.

Dacia traced the edges of his face, sending a warm, tingling sensation through his entire being. Then she moved to his scalp, gently combing her fingers through his hair.

He had wanted her to touch him like this for so long. He prayed that it wasn't a hallucination brought on by the painkillers. He prayed that it was real and that when he opened his eyes, she would still be there with him. Touching his face.

As Cody faded into sleep, he heard her laugh. The sound seemed off, but he couldn't pry his eyes open. The medication dragged him under.

Dacia gasped.

The sound immediately pulled Cody from his dreams of her and him. Were they real? Had he asked her to be his? "What's wrong, Dacia?"

"Your face is, uh…" She waved her hand in front of him.

"Is beat up, I know." He couldn't keep the irritation from his voice. It had been a dream, nothing more. Just a wonderful, unforgettable dream. "Did you forget?"

"No, that's just it." Her eyes widened when she shook her head. "It's not anymore."

"What do you mean?" He didn't intend to come off so gruff. He needed to calm down. It wasn't her fault that he'd imagined them together.

"I was running my fingers through your hair, wishing that this hadn't happened to you."

She'd been running her hand through his hair? Was it … could it be real? His insides fluttered, and for a moment, he felt light enough to fly.

She was still talking. He focused on her, not wanting to miss a thing she said. "And all of your bruises and cuts began disappearing before my eyes. I thought I was seeing things. I fell asleep, and when I woke up … well, you look great. I don't know what else to say."

Clasping his hands behind his head, he stared at the wall for a while, wondering if he should ask about the kiss. If it had happened, it would be easy enough to explain why he wasn't sure if it had. If it hadn't, he would look like a total idiot. "Another power. Bet that's why your face healed so fast."

She rubbed her cheek. "I don't know. I figured it disappeared because there was no way it ever could've happened to begin with. I never considered any other options. Oh." She lifted her hand to her mouth, covering it. "Maybe you'll get out of here today."

"That'd be nice. Sick of lying here—" he paused for a moment, hoping this was the right opportunity to ask without asking "—although, I'm enjoying the company."

"Yeah, the company's good." She smiled, and a blush covered her cheeks. "It's just too bad it took something like this to make us realize we should be together."

His stomach seemed to be doing cartwheels, but he tried to school his face to stay calm. "Thought about it since Falcon Lake. Sitting with you felt good, but you didn't seem interested." Oh, so gently, he reached out and traced a fingertip along her cheek. It was real. She was real.

Goosebumps rose on her arms, and he smiled like a fool. Seeing her react to his touch this way filled him with a sense of satisfaction.

"I've been thinking about it too much. Every time you hold my hand or touch me, but Cody—" Her voice cracked.

"What?"

"You deserve so much better."

"Da—"

"Things like this are going to keep happening. People are scared of me, and it's going to affect you." She lifted his arm over her shoulders and rested her head on his chest. Then she took his other hand in hers.

"It's worth it," he mumbled into her hair.

The remaining clouds disappeared, and the room brightened.

"Samantha'll be back soon." Cody pulled her closer, expecting a shooting pain through his ribs, but it didn't come. "Do we tell her?"

She sat up. "I'll tell her on our way back to campus." A huge smile spread over her face, and Cody's chest warmed at the sight. Seeing her happy was all he wanted.

At first, Cody thought she was standing up, then he realized that she was floating off the bed, sitting at least six inches above the blanket.

"Oh, crap." She hit the mattress with a thump and stood up.

His eyes crinkled at the corners, and a grin spread across his face. "What was that?"

Heat rushed up her neck and onto her cheeks. "Happiness." She took a step back.

He snatched her hand, keeping her from moving farther away. He wanted her right next to him. "Don't be embarrassed." His voice was soft and low. He didn't want to spook her. He was terrified she would change her mind about them being together. "I'd fly right now if I could."

He didn't get a chance to find out if he had calmed her or not. The door opened as soon as the words were out of his mouth, and Samantha walked into the room carrying a flower arrangement.

As soon as her gaze met Cody's, the vase slipped through her fingers, crashing against the floor, and shattering into a thousand pieces. "Oh, wow, I guess you don't need 'Get Well' flowers anymore. Do you?"

"No, Dacia has healing powers." Cody looked up into Dacia's face, and realizing he still clutched her arm, he dropped his hand. "She's the best doctor ever. Thanks, though. Was a nice thought."

Samantha stared down at the broken flowers and shards of glass. "I've got to find someone to clean this up. Will you come with me, Dacia?"

Dacia nodded. "Sure." She stepped around the mess on the floor and followed Samantha into the hallway. The door swung shut behind them.

Cody lay back against the pillows and let out a contented sigh. He'd asked, and she'd said yes. He knew she deserved better, but he would work hard to be good enough, strong enough for her.

They were only out of the room for a couple of minutes before Samantha held the door open and said, "You can go back in with Lover Boy if you want."

"Thanks." Dacia practically skipped back to Cody's side. "Samantha knows. She could tell something was up."

Judging by what he'd heard, he assumed she was happy for Dacia, but wanting to be sure, he asked, "What'd she say?"

"She said everyone but us has known for a long time that we should be together."

"Least we know now." He grabbed her hand and pulled her toward him. She settled on his bed again, sitting with one leg dangling over the edge and the other leaning against him. He held onto her thigh, wondering how such a horrible day had ended up being so good.

When the door opened again, neither of them looked toward it.

"What is this mess?" A deep, male voice broke through the silence, startling Cody and making Dacia jump.

A man that couldn't have been any older than his mid-thirties looked down at the shattered vase. He was wearing blue scrubs under a white lab coat.

"Our friend is finding someone to clean it up." Dacia hopped up. "She was a bit stunned by Cody's quick recovery."

"She should be more careful. Somebody could get hurt." The man still hadn't looked up from the mess. "So, what's this improvement?" He turned toward Cody, and the chart he'd been holding slipped from his fingers, crashing to the floor. It clattered against the tiles barely missing the water from the flowers. His jaw dropped open, and he stared at Cody for what seemed like an eternity. His green gaze traveled from the top of Cody's head to his toes and then over him again. "How did this … when did … what's going on?"

Cody's eyes flashed to the man's nametag: David Sequoia, M.D. He didn't look like any doctor that Cody had ever been seen by before. He'd always had doctors that were old enough they could have been his parents. This guy looked like one of the doctors on the TV shows: six feet tall, auburn hair, and green eyes. The girls that watched those dramas would've loved him.

"We don't know, doctor, but it's pretty amazing." Cody shrugged. "I feel like a new man."

Dacia picked up the chart and handed it to the doctor before standing behind one of the chairs. "Now you know why my friend dropped the flowers."

"Yes, I guess I can understand." He stepped up to the bed and pushed Cody's hair back, studying his forehead. "Even the gash on your face is gone." He looked over Cody, searching for any trace of his injuries. He pressed on Cody's ribs. "Does that hurt at all?"

When he said that, scenes from the emergency room flashed through Cody's mind. His voice triggered the memories. Cody hadn't been able to see him through his swollen eyes, but the compassion in his voice was the same as it had been.

"No, sir."

"I can't imagine how you could've healed so fast. It doesn't make any sense." He flipped through Cody's chart and rubbed his jaw. "I'm taking you back to x-ray. I want to see new films."

Cody shrugged. He actually felt sorry for the guy. He had to think he was going crazy, but there was nothing Cody could do about it, except pretend like he had no idea what had happened. "Sure, Doc, but I feel fine."

Dr. Sequoia inhaled deeply, then slowly blew out his breath. "I'll send Nurse Cypress in with a wheelchair. We'll take some x-rays and see what's going on with you."

Samantha walked into the room, and her cheeks flushed. "Sorry about the mess," she said as she passed by the doctor. "It took me a while to find someone to clean it up."

His smile was off, distorted by his disbelief. "Don't worry. If I'd had flowers, I'd be in the same predicament."

"Dropped my chart instead." Cody nodded at the floor.

"The nurse will be in soon." The door closed with a snick behind Dr. Sequoia.

Samantha hooked her thumb toward the sound. "Is it just me or does he seem grumpy?"

"Confused." Cody rubbed the mattress beside him, hoping that with Samantha in the room Dacia would feel comfortable enough to sit there again. "His bedside manner was much better this morning."

"I imagine." Samantha laughed. "He probably thinks he stepped into the Twilight Zone."

Dacia situated herself next to him. "Samantha and I can wait until you get back from x-ray. Then we should head back to campus." She rubbed her thumb under his eye, staring down at him. "It might've been better for you if I'd waited to heal you until you were out of here."

"No," he said. "I hate hospitals. Now, hopefully, I'll be out tomorrow."

She twisted a lock of her hair around her finger, a nervous habit she'd had since the first day he'd met her. "I know, but they'll want an explanation."

"If they need one"—Samantha shrugged—"they'll just have to settle for a miracle."

"Not like you meant to." Cody pulled her hand free from her hair, sliding his fingers through hers. The motion was so natural already. Granted, when they were friends, he had held her hand several times, but this felt different than that had. This felt as instinctual as breathing.

There was a knock on the door before the janitor came in to clean up the flowers. As soon as he finished, Tammy came in. She waved at the wheelchair. "Your chariot awaits." She moved the IV stand before helping Cody to his feet.

He sat up and slid his splinted leg over the edge of the bed. Unable to bend it, it stuck straight out in front of him. Pressing both of his hands down on the mattress he pushed himself up, keeping his weight off his injured leg. He leaned on Tammy, letting her bear some of his bulk just in case his knee gave out. He gingerly set his foot on the ground, putting a little bit of pressure on it, testing to see how sturdy it was.

It felt as good as new. No twinges. No stabbing pain.

He lifted his other foot off the floor and looked over his shoulder at Dacia, shooting her a smile. As he sat in the chair, he realized he was only wearing a hospital gown. His cheeks burned as Tammy wheeled him out of the room. He hoped his butt hadn't been hanging out when he stood up.

"I've never seen anything like this," Tammy said as she backed his chair into the elevator. "Your healing is nothing short of miraculous." She pushed the button, and the door slid closed. "I don't know if you have any idea how awful you looked this morning, but, honey, it was bad."

Cody closed his eyes. He didn't want to be injured still, but he didn't want this kind of attention either. "Felt bad."

"I didn't think you would ever walk right again," she continued on, apparently not noticing his discomfort. "That would've been terrible. Obviously, you're very athletic, and to have something like this happen at such a young age, would just be devastating." She rambled on and on, not pausing to let him respond, and that's when he realized that he made her nervous. She had never seen anything like this before, and she couldn't comprehend it.

He'd been scared by Dacia's powers, so he understood what Tammy was going through. Looking up at her, he smiled and nodded.

At 7:50, Tammy brought Cody back to the room. "My shift's done in ten minutes," she said. "I'll be back at 8:00 in the morning."

"Thanks." Cody tried to keep the irritation out of his voice but failed miserably. It wasn't her fault that they had redone his x-rays three times or taken most of his blood. It wasn't her fault that his stomach was growling angrily. He hopped out of the wheelchair, grateful to have the splint off of his leg, plopped down on the bed, crossed his arms tightly, and glared at the door.

"Well …" Samantha said.

"Said they were taking me to x-ray. They poked and prodded me." He started to get out of bed but stopped. He needed sweatpants or shorts or something to wear under this stupid gown. Instead of standing, he threw his arms up. "Took tons of blood. Surprised they didn't take samples of my brain tissue."

"I'm sorry, Cody." Dacia chewed on her bottom lip and stared down at the floor. "I didn't mean to put you through this."

"It's okay, Dacia." Not wanting her to feel guilty, he let out a gust of air, trying to calm himself. "Rather be annoyed than feel like earlier. 'Sides, now, I can open my eyes and see you." Grabbing her hand, he pulled her toward him. His anger diminished as soon as his fingers touched hers.

"Aww, isn't that sweet?" Samantha snickered. "I think I'm gonna puke."

Dacia rolled her eyes at Samantha.

"What? Somebody's got to tease the two of you."

"Yeah, yeah, yeah." Cody massaged his temples with the hand that wasn't holding Dacia's. "The verdict: I'm not broken. Missing a lotta blood I came with. Figured I'd lost enougha that."

"Yeah," Dacia said in a husky voice. "I'd have to agree with that."

He smiled up at her. "Get to leave tomorrow."

Samantha walked to the door. "I'm going to get out of here and let the two of you say goodbye. You don't need me standing around making you feel uncomfortable." She turned and looked at Cody. "I'd tell you to get some rest so you can get better, but I think that's been taken care of."

Dacia sat on the side of the bed and ran her fingers through Cody's hair. "I'm sorry this had to happen." She scrunched her nose up, and Cody wondered how bad he smelled. It had been a long day, and he could use a shower. "I'd better go. Samantha's waiting on me. Don't forget to call your parents."

"Yeah." He sighed. At least Sarah hadn't gotten ahold of them earlier. What would they think of his miraculous recovery?

"They should be home by now."

He fisted his hands and relaxed them over and over again. "What do I say? I'm fine."

"I don't know." She looked at the door.

"Better go." His voice softened, and he looked up at her, hoping she could see the concern in his eyes. "Watch your back 'til I can." He squeezed her hand one more time, not wanting to let go. "Know you can take care of yourself. Did a better job than me, but I worry."

Her eyes had a glossy look to them. "Thanks, Cody."

Reaching up, he brushed his knuckles over her cheek. Then he cupped the back of her head, pulling her mouth down to his.

The kiss made his lips tingle long after she left.

Chapter 11

Dream Come True

Cody sat on the bed, staring at his cell phone. He had a signal here. He had wi-fi. He had no reason not to call his parents.

But what was he supposed to say?

Finally, deciding that they might not believe him unless they could see him, he made a video call.

"Hey, Mom," Cody said when she answered.

Her face brightened instantly. "It's so good to see you. Where are you that you have service?"

"I'm okay." He needed her to understand that first. He walked around, panning the room with his phone. "Hospital."

She gasped, and Cody turned the phone so they could see each other again. "Is this why the school called? What happened? Do you need me there?"

"Breathe, Mom." He tried to laugh, but it sounded as phony as it felt. "Remember I'm okay." He'd been thinking about this since Dacia left and had settled on flat out lying. He intentionally held the phone at a bad angle so that she couldn't see his face clearly. "Thought maybe it was a kidney stone, but I'm better. Going home tomorrow."

"Oh, honey." Her mouth drooped, and he knew she wanted to be with him, to help him, to mom him, but if his dad was on a business trip, she couldn't come. She needed to be there with his younger siblings. "Is there anything I can do? Do you need anything? Are you there all alone?"

He sat on the bed and adjusted it to the perfect position. "Dacia was here most of the day." The grin spread over his face before he could stop it. There was no sense not telling her. She would figure it out now. "We're together."

"Well, it's about time." She shook her head at the phone. "I have no idea what took you so long."

"Me either, Mom." He should've expected that reaction. "Me either."

Cody stood in front of the window, staring out at the mountains in the distance, waiting for Dacia to rescue him. Doctors and nurses had started showing up in his room early this morning. They took him for more blood tests and x-rays. They did a CT scan. He tried to be understanding, but he was nearing the end of his patience. They weren't going to find anything, and they should have realized that by now. He wanted Dacia to get here, so he didn't have to face another doctor or nurse or test if he didn't have to.

When the door opened again, he spun around and stood rigid, ready for a confrontation, but it was her. When she saw him, she stumbled back and pressed her hand to her heart.

His expression softened, and he strode across the room to Dacia.

"Hey." She cleared the roughness from her throat. "How are you doing?"

"Thought you were another doctor wanting to run tests." Cody pulled her against him. He held her, never wanting to let go, rubbing his hands over her back.

Dropping the bag she'd been holding, she embraced him, buried her head in his chest, and sniffled.

Cody stepped back, still holding onto her. He rested his forehead against hers and stared into her wet eyes. "What's wrong?" He rubbed her arm in a barely-there caress.

"I … I had a dream." Her words were softer than a whisper.

He focused on listening to what she was saying and not all the other sounds in the room.

"They came here and left you on the floor," she said everything so quickly that the words blended together. "You were broken, and nobody knew you needed help." Her fingers dug through the thin gown into his skin, clutching him.

He brushed her hair back and kissed her forehead. "It's okay," he murmured. "I'm here."

"I couldn't go back to sleep." She chewed on her lip, and it was obvious to him that she didn't want to say whatever came next. "I didn't plan on it." She took a deep breath. "I got in my truck and drove here. I needed to see you. I needed to know you were okay." She looked up at him. Her face was set. She was ready for him to tell her it was stupid. She was ready for a fight.

"Never came." She might be ready for a fight, but he wasn't. Not with her. Not right now.

She shook her head. "No. There was something in the road. I lost control." She shuddered and clenched his hospital gown in her fists. "It was him. He made me wreck." Her knees weakened, and she slumped against him.

He held her. Thanking God for letting her be here with him. He could've lost her. The thought made his chest ache.

"My truck—" a sob tore free from her throat "—hit a tree. The airbag exploded." Her tears soaked through his gown. "I woke up this morning. There was blood everywhere."

He stepped back and held her out at arm's length, looking her over from head to toe. She seemed fine, but he had to be missing something.

"Not a scratch." She smiled at him through her tears. "Nothing. I healed. I have no idea how bad or even what it was. I know that I shouldn't have gone out by myself, but I wanted to see you. I was so scared." She collapsed against his chest and sobbed.

He held her, one hand caressing her head, the other wrapped around her.

When she was all cried out, she backed away from him. "I'm sorry." She turned her face away, staring out the window. "I don't know what came over me."

Cody folded his arms over his chest and rolled his eyes. "Could be saving the world, finding me beaten, or wrecking your truck. Don't be sorry. There's nothing wrong with crying."

"There is when it's all you do …"

"You held up yesterday."

"I wanted to be strong for you." She reached for his hand, and he took hold of it. "I didn't want you to know how worried I was or how awful you looked."

He never would have gotten through yesterday without her. Didn't she know that? She had been his rock. His hope. The one person who could pull him out of his despair. "Probably why you needed to let it out today."

"Maybe."

He pulled her close. She fit perfectly against him like they had been made for each other. He rested his head on hers and felt complete.

She tilted her head, and her lips brushed against his. Cody's breath hitched. Suddenly, there was nothing in the world except the two of them. He moved his mouth against hers, and when she responded, he deepened the kiss. His hands splayed over her back. Heat surged through his body. She ran her fingers up his arms, and his muscles tightened beneath her touch.

The door creaked. Dacia stepped back, but Cody didn't let go of her waist. His thumbs rubbed over the soft fabric of her t-shirt. Her cheeks were bright red, and her emerald eyes sparkled in the light shining in through the window.

"Excuse me," the nurse said.

Cody's hands tightened. "My ride's here. No more tests." He glanced at Dacia. "Let's go."

"As cute as I think you are in that gown, maybe you should change." She picked up the bag she'd carried in. "I brought some clothes."

A self-conscious smile crept over his face. "Yeah … thanks."

The nurse left the room without another word. Cody bent down and brushed his lips over Dacia's, then grabbed the bag, and went to the bathroom to get dressed.

He hurriedly pulled on the socks, jeans, t-shirt, and hoodie that she'd brought for him. The clothes he'd worn to the hospital had been cut off of him, but they'd saved his shoes. He walked out of the bathroom, slipped them on, and grabbed his other belongings. Then he walked over to Dacia. He stood next to her, watching her for several seconds. She stared out of the window, but he didn't think she was seeing anything there. A peaceful expression covered her face. He didn't want to disturb her, but he didn't want to wait around for another doctor or nurse to come in. "You ready?"

She blinked rapidly. "Yeah."

"What were you thinking?" He moved his hand closer to hers but left a breath of air between them.

She shrugged, making him even more curious.

"Must've been good. You had a sweet smile." Aching to touch her, he brushed a strand of hair off of her forehead. "So, what was it?"

"Nothing." Red spread from her neck and over her face and ears.

"That wasn't nothing." He tilted his head to the side and looked at her with puppy-dog eyes. "I thought couples weren't supposed to have secrets."

"I suppose you're right." She grinned at him, and there was a mischievous hint to it that he wasn't used to seeing there. "One of the paramedics who brought you in here yesterday was really cute." She held onto Cody's arms and stood on her tip-toes, looking toward the door. "I wonder if he's here today."

"Ouch, did you hear that?" He grabbed his chest. He was glad that Dacia felt good enough to tease him. "That was my heart breaking."

She giggled and rolled her eyes at him. "Actually, I was thinking you made me pretty happy yesterday when you, uh, well, kinda sorta, well, umm, asked me to, uh, go out with you. I think you made me the happiest I've ever been."

Warmth spread through him, bringing a smile to his face, and softening his voice. "Yeah, made me happy when you agreed. Doesn't mean you can make fun of my speech."

"Somebody has to." She latched onto his hand, squeezing his fingers. "Might as well be me."

As soon as they stepped outside, Dacia handed him his keys. "I don't want to drive."

Cody pulled out of the parking lot and followed the streets through Althea toward the curvy mountain road that led to Phlox University. He held Dacia's hand over the console.

Lodgepole pines crowded together on the shoulders, stretching to the heavens. As they climbed higher, the trees became sparser. In some areas, there were grand views of the mountains. In one of these areas, Dacia let go of his hand, clutched her throat, and gasped.

"What's wrong? Are you okay?" Cody glanced at her quickly before looking back at the road. He reached for her hand. Her skin was colder than it had been just moments before.

"If I hadn't healed, nobody would've found me for days." Her voice trembled. "I'd have died."

"If I'd've known, I'd've been looking for you last night." Fear tightened Cody's gut and clawed at his throat. He'd been so close to losing her, and he hadn't even known. How could he keep her safe? Even if she didn't have a demon after her, how could he protect her?

"Nobody knew where I was going." She rubbed her forehead and stared out the window. "Nobody would've found me."

Squeezing her hand, he looked over at her. Her shoulders were slumped, and her right hand was wrapped around her stomach. "Glad you're all right, but don't do that again. Don't go anywhere alone."

"I know." She dropped her head to her chest. "It was stupid, but it's better for me to be alone than you ... and maybe even Samantha."

Cody tightened his grip on the steering wheel, making the tendons in his hands and forearms bulge. "That won't happen again." He worked hard not to hate, trying to remember that most people had something they were dealing with. It was something his parents had instilled in him, something they did. He wanted to be like them in that aspect, but right now, he hated Alvin, Cassandra, Vanessa, and Bryce, and he didn't know if he would ever be able to forgive them for what they'd done to him, but more than that, he couldn't forgive them for what they'd wanted to do to her.

They remained silent for the rest of the trip, holding hands and dealing with their personal demons. Cody gently rubbed his thumb along Dacia's, comforting himself and hopefully her at the same time.

He put the car in park and stared at the dorm. Right there. He'd been right there when they attacked him. Later in the day, somebody might have noticed, but early in the morning a lot of students were still sleeping.

Dacia slid her hand onto Cody's thigh. Some of his tension eased. He didn't look away from the bushes when he said, "Rain probably washed all the blood away."

"Probably," she agreed.

He shook his head. Thanks to Dacia he was all right. There was no sense in dwelling on it. He couldn't go back and change things. He got out of his car and turned his back on the shrubs, hoping to put the incident behind him.

Dacia slid her hand into his, threading their fingers together, and they walked toward the building. She opened the door to her room, and before they stepped over the threshold, Samantha fisted her hands on her hips and glowered at them. "Did Dacia tell you what she did last night?"

Wow. He'd never seen her so angry. "She told me, and I let her have it." His lips twitched, threatening to expose his exaggeration.

"She told you?" Samantha's mouth hung open. "I can't believe she told you. She must've felt really guilty."

"Yes, I told him." Cody could practically hear the eye roll in Dacia's tone. "You do realize I'm standing here in the room with you, don't you?"

Samantha's hands dropped from her hips. "I can't believe she told you."

"Hello." Dacia waved her hands in the air. "I'm right here. I figured he would find out when we left the hospital in his car instead of my truck."

"Oh, yeah"—Samantha looked up out of the corner of her eyes—"I guess that might have made him wonder what was going on."

"Thanks for telling on me, though." Dacia crossed her arms over her chest and smirked at Samantha.

"Well, ladies, if you're done fighting, I'm starving." Cody rubbed his stomach. "Do either of you want to come along?"

Samantha and Dacia looked at each other and smiled. "Of course, we do." Samantha grabbed her jacket and started for the door.

When they were almost to Sedum Student Center, Dacia's steps faltered. "The Potato Heads might be confused by your speedy recovery if they're in the cafeteria."

"Maybe they'll back off." Cody's voice hardened. "Half the school probably knows I went to the hospital, but not gonna hide 'til this blows over." His breath sounded so loud to him. He caught himself clenching his jaw again and tried to relax his muscles, but they just kept tightening.

"I don't expect you to hide out or pretend like you're still injured." Dacia brushed her knuckles against the back of his hand. "I just wanted to remind you before we walk into the cafeteria."

"I know." His upper lip pulled up on one side.

"We're going to have to come up with a story so we're all on the same page," Dacia said as he held the door open for her and Samantha.

Cody let out a deep breath, and his hand trembled. He hurriedly stepped inside before losing his grip on the door.

Samantha, being sensible and level-headed, said, "Maybe they won't be around until after their hearing."

He should have thought of that, but he couldn't think straight when it came to them anymore. He wished he could talk to his parents about this and get their insight, but as far as they knew, he had a kidney stone.

He filled his plate. The chicken tenders that he'd split with Dacia at the hospital hadn't been enough to satiate him for this long. He'd had every intention of eating breakfast this morning, but the doctors and nurses had kept him away from his room until the food was ice cold.

The three of them sat at a table against the back that was half-hidden by a partial wall. He hoped it would keep people from noticing him. Even though he didn't want to hide, he also didn't want to be the center of attention.

"Justin and Dan are coming over," Samantha whispered across the table.

Cody's lips tightened into a thin line, but by the time his buddies reached the table, he'd managed to stifle all outward appearance of tension. They nodded at each other in that way that guys do.

Justin grabbed the back of a chair but didn't sit. His deep brown eyes swept over Cody. "I heard you were in the hospital." His black eyebrows pulled together, making creases on his forehead.

"Spent the night there." Cody sipped his drink. His hand shook, but he didn't think anyone else noticed.

Dacia rubbed his thigh, and the movement took his focus off of Justin and Dan. Instead of worrying about what they would say, he remembered kissing her and holding her like he'd wanted to for so long. He glanced down at her fingers, drawing circles over his jeans. "Dacia just brought me back."

"What happened?" Dan's auburn eyebrows drew together. "Drew said Dacia stopped by this morning but didn't have too much to say. You look fine to me."

"Kidney stone." Since he had to lie, he figured he should use the same one with everybody. It would be easier to keep track of that way. "You guys up for a game?"

Justin and Dan looked at each other and shrugged. "Sure … when?" Justin asked.

"3:30." He knew Dacia would worry about it being during her lesson, but he couldn't hide. He needed to live his life. He would just have to be more careful now.

"We'll get Drew and round up a couple of other guys. See you on the court." Justin turned and left.

"Later, Dacia … Samantha," Dan said Dacia's name first, but he never looked away from Samantha.

It was obvious that she noticed his attention because her face grew redder by the second.

"See ya." Dacia turned toward Samantha and raised an eyebrow.

Samantha shook her head and nodded at Cody. He didn't think he was supposed to notice, so he pretended not to.

"Guess I got outta that one … for now." Cody's shoulders relaxed, and he released a deep breath.

Samantha finished her salad, took a long drink of her water, and said, "Well, I'm going to get out of here. Be careful at your lesson, Dacia, and be careful playing basketball, Cody. Keep your eyes open."

"You too." He nodded at her, holding her gaze with his. Dacia had had nightmares that killed off both him and Sarah. He couldn't help but wonder if Samantha would be next.

"I will for real this time," Dacia said. As soon as Samantha got up, Dacia smiled at Cody. "Well, I guess she thought we should have some time alone."

"Nothing wrong with that." He hooked his fingers under her chair and dragged her closer.

She moved her hands to the table, possibly in an effort to balance herself. He reached up and placed his over them. "In fact"—he leaned in—"don't mind at all. Sam's great, but nice to be alone." He turned her chair so that her legs were between his. "Haven't had much time since high school."

"No, we haven't."

Her breath caressed his face, sending shivers through his body. To be this close to her and to have her want it as much as he did was the best thing that had ever happened to him.

"But I have to admit, it's nice to have a female friend for a change." She lifted her legs over his and pulled his arm around her shoulders, snuggling up against him. He traced small circles on her skin.

Chapter 12

Control

$\mathcal{D}$acia and Cody strolled to Sarah's office. His arm was draped over her shoulders, and hers was wrapped around his waist. Sitting with her tucked up against his side had released most of his tension. Since he didn't expect any trouble from the Potato Heads until after their hearing, he decided to enjoy this time with Dacia.

When they reached Cacomistle Hall, Dacia's face paled. "She isn't going to be happy with me."

"Brought it on yourself." Cody held the door open for her.

Dacia waved at Alicia as the two of them headed for the massive open staircase. They stood outside of Sarah's door. Dacia held her hand in the air, waiting to knock.

Cody wasn't going to rush her. He put his hand on her shoulder, hoping to give her strength. Taking a deep breath, she knocked, and not waiting for an answer, they stepped inside.

"Hello." Sarah sat on the couch. Her legs were crossed, and a folder was open on her lap. She stared at Cody for a long moment before smiling brightly at him. "You look amazing, Cody. Maybe Dacia should think about medical school."

Her lip curled in disgust. "Maybe, but I don't like blood and gore."

"She'll be good at anything she does." Cody kissed her cheek. "Don't leave without me."

Blood rushed to Dacia's face.

"Cody"—Sarah pointed at the couch—"have a seat."

Cody and Dacia sat next to each other, and he pulled her against his side. He wasn't looking forward to this conversation, but at least he had Dacia next to him.

The faint lines on Sarah's face deepened, showing her annoyance. "I suspended your attackers until next week."

"Right." Cody kept his voice clipped, hoping not to show any emotion whatsoever.

"The Board of Trustees will meet Friday morning to decide on their punishment." She got up and walked behind the couch she'd been sitting on. "I have no control over the board. I can offer suggestions, but I cannot make the decision or contend it."

"What will you recommend?" Dacia fisted her hands on her lap.

"Expulsion." Sarah's face contorted, showing a side of her that Cody had never seen. "They could've killed you both." She waved her arm in their direction. "Not that you can see that now."

Unintentionally, Cody tightened his grip on Dacia's arm, relaxing it a bit as soon as he realized what he'd done. "But …"

"But …" She sucked in a deep breath, and her shoulders slumped. "The board won't believe the extent of your injuries, and Cassandra's mother is one of the members."

Cody felt his pulse ramp up. From the time his wounds healed, he'd expected this would be the outcome, but anger boiled inside of him like magma that was ready to erupt. "They're going to get away with it." He pulled his arm out from behind Dacia and leaned forward on his steepled fingertips.

"Most likely." Sarah nodded, and her lips pinched together into a thin line. "You can file assault charges with the police, but I imagine, with no injuries, the results will be the same."

Dacia ran her hand up and down his back. "They won't stop."

"No, probably not." Sarah looked weary.

"They'll attack Dacia next." Cody closed his eyes and rubbed his forehead.

Sarah's head flinched back slightly before she focused on Dacia. "Did you happen to mention to Cody what they did to you yesterday?"

He jerked to an upright position and stared at her with wide eyes. Something had happened and she hadn't told him? Why hadn't he asked? He knew they were planning on going after her next. Obviously, they had. "What happened? Why didn't you say anything?"

"Well, I, uh …" She dragged her fingers through her hair and held them there for a few seconds before pulling through a knot at the end. "With everything that happened, it kind of slipped my mind."

He lifted his hands and jiggled his head from side to side. "It's on your mind now."

"I spaced off when I was waiting for you." She leaned forward with her elbows on her knees and rubbed her hands together. A soft chafing noise accompanied her words. "When I opened the door, they grabbed me, and Vanessa shoved a rag in my mouth."

Cody closed his eyes and winced. Each word felt like a punch in his gut. He should have been there for her. He should have been stronger.

"Bryce told me not to try anything and it would all be over quickly."

Cody's ears burned as the magma inside of him became more unstable. He rolled his neck, trying to relax. She was here next to him. She was okay.

"Cassandra whispered in my ear that they had taken care of you." Dacia swallowed. "Bryce and Alvin dragged me down the hallway. There was a bulletin board hanging on the wall, so I closed my eyes and used my magic to pull it off and into Bryce's injured hand. It worked, but he didn't let go."

Cody reached up and massaged Dacia's neck. The movement reminded him that she was here with him, that whatever had happened she was okay.

"When I opened my eyes, I saw Cassandra's fist flying at my face. I didn't have time to dodge it." She rubbed her jaw as if remembering the pain. "They dragged me to the stairs. Cassandra and Vanessa grabbed my feet and lifted me. I kicked out, but Bryce yanked my arm, pulling me backward. They swung me before throwing me down the stairs."

Cody ground his teeth together so hard that he wondered if they would shatter.

She looked at him and smiled. It was genuine, and he couldn't figure out what there was to smile about. "I flew. They were terrified, like mice standing before a lion." She squeezed his knee. "I held my hand out, and a small flame rose from my palm. I asked them where you were, and they wouldn't tell me, so I let it grow. Vanessa was so scared. She finally caved. As soon as she told me where they'd thrown you, I could picture you."

Cody's muscles were rigid. The anger that had been building inside of him needed an outlet, but he didn't want to explode here. He needed to get away.

She rubbed his leg. "I'm okay, Cody. I got away from them, and I had more control than ever." She turned toward Sarah, pulling her hand away. "I'm hoping that will transfer into my lessons today."

He let some of his rage go, and when he spoke, his voice was tortured. "I should've been there to protect you." He turned away, rubbing his neck. "And since when can you control your powers like that?"

She placed her hand on his knee again. The relief her touch brought was almost instantaneous. "I can't. Knowing you were hurt was the catalyst."

"You had quite a day yesterday," Sarah said. "Your control was very impressive."

Dacia tilted her head to the side and shook it. "I didn't do so well at the hospital."

"What happened?" Cody turned on the couch so that his knee was between them.

She sucked in a deep breath, then covered her mouth with her hands. "I nearly boiled a bottle of water, and I started several storms."

He nodded. The heavy sheets of rain. The thunder and lightning. "Remember the storms."

"Yes." At some point, Sarah had set the folder on the couch beside her. She fiddled with it now. "But for the most part, you had outstanding control."

"I gotta go." Cody stood and looked down at Dacia. He wanted to stay here. He wanted to be there for her, but he had to show up to that game. If he didn't, there would be even more rumors. "I've got a game to get to. Be back around 5:00."

Dacia grabbed hold of his hand and walked him to the door. "I know this is your line, but *please* be careful."

"Promise." He bent down and pressed his lips to hers, a promise for more to come. "Later."

Chapter 13

Fire And Ice

Cody reached for the knob, and the door swung open. "Hello, Cody," Sarah said as she stepped to the side.

"Better get used to this." Cody looked from his hand still in the air to Dacia. He tilted his head, and his eyebrows pinched together. "Yesterday, why didn't you realize it wasn't me at your door?"

"Uh, good question." She lifted one of her shoulders to her ear and sat there for a minute. "I don't know for sure. I was staring out the window, waiting for you to come, and I sort of spaced out. When they knocked on the door, I hesitated for a moment but opened it anyway."

"Don't sense me, don't open." Cody tucked his hands into his pockets. He felt the heat rising inside of him again and didn't want Dacia to think it was her that he was mad at.

"That's a good idea." Sarah nodded at Cody, then looked at Dacia to make sure she understood. "It never occurred to me to ask that."

Dacia yawned, and her head bobbed forward. "I'm not used to it yet." Her eyes drifted closed, and it took her a few seconds to open them back up again. "If I'd been sensing people's approach for the last five years, maybe I'd've thought about it, but I only sense Cody and only for the last couple of days."

"Just do me a favor and think about it." Cody walked over and put his hand on Dacia's shoulder. "So, how was the lesson?"

"She was very impressive today." Sarah sat up straighter and beamed at Dacia.

"Oh, really." Cody grinned down at her. He had no doubt that she would get this. She was smart and determined. Figuring out her powers wouldn't be any different than any other challenge she'd faced. "What'd you do?"

"Would you like to see?" Before he had a chance to respond, a blue ball of fire formed in her palm.

"Wicked." Cody stared, not pulling his gaze from the flames that flickered and danced on her hand, not quite touching her skin but hovering just above it.

The fireball grew in her palm until it was the size of a grapefruit. She held it there, not looking away while she pulled her hand from underneath it. The flames hung in the air.

Cody's eyes widened and he mouthed, "Wow."

"That's only the beginning," Sarah told him as she too stared at the flames.

Dacia held her hand in front of it, and ice shot from her fingertips, engulfing the fire, fighting for dominance. The ice devoured the flames, suffocating them, turning them into a globe. She levitated it, floating it to Cody.

The icy ball hung in the air in front of him. He reached for it, hesitating to grab it. Finally, he snatched it up and turned it, staring into it where the ice still consumed the flames. "Saaa-weet!"

"Well, everybody has to be good at something." Dacia slumped back against the couch. "I can turn fire into ice. That should get me far in life. Don't you think?"

"It just might," Sarah murmured.

Cody looked at her, wondering if she thought that was the answer to defeating Nefarious.

Dacia ignored the comment. "So, when do we meet again?"

"Tomorrow afternoon."

Dacia stood and immediately fell, barely catching herself on the arm of the couch.

"Dacia—" Cody grabbed her just above the elbow and helped her back onto the sofa "—are you okay?"

She yawned, showing Cody and Sarah her tonsils. "I don't know what's wrong with me, but I'm exhausted."

Sarah rubbed her chin, not looking away from Dacia. "I wonder if using your powers takes some kind of toll. You've used them a lot today."

"And yesterday." Cody watched her, hoping the answer could be that simple. It seemed logical, no different than a muscle.

Dacia's chin fell forward, hitting her chest. She shook her head and opened her eyes wider than necessary. "Yesterday, when I was healing Cody, I fell asleep, so—" she yawned again "—it could've been sapping my strength."

"Stay here until you're ready to leave." Sarah nodded at the couch. "I've got some work to do in my office."

"Thanks." Cody sat next to Dacia, and she laid her head on his shoulder. "Sleep if you need to."

"Maybe for a few minutes." She pulled her feet up onto the couch and curled against him.

Cody rubbed circles on her arm while she drifted off. Her breathing evened out, and he marveled at the fact that she was there with him, sleeping in his arms.

After an hour or more, Cody gently nudged her awake. They left Sarah's office hand in hand but not before Dacia grabbed a couple of books off the coffee table.

As soon as they stepped outside, the fresh air rejuvenated him. The sky was a brilliant blue. Poufy clouds drifted across it. Fall leaves littered the ground, crunching beneath their feet.

"What's with the books?" Cody draped his arm over her shoulders. "Sarah giving you homework?"

"Not exactly, one of them is Sarah's grandfather's journal. The other is an older journal written in Latin. While Sarah and I talked about them, I felt an overwhelming need to bring them back with me." Her hands trembled. "Maybe I'll learn something about Nefarious from them. I don't know."

He hated seeing her like this. Dacia had always had to hide her quirks from everyone, but one of the things he'd admired about her was her ability to not lose faith in others. He wished that she had that same faith in herself. "It'll work out. The sun always rises in the morning and always sets at night. Nothing is going to change that." He pulled her closer. "I know you're worried, but you'll figure out a way."

"Thanks, but I don't think so." She sounded so broken.

"You need a break." He wanted to help her somehow, and nature had always rejuvenated her in the past. "Let's go to Falcon Lake."

She stopped so suddenly that it jerked his arm. "Aren't you worried about getting jumped again?"

"Why?" Something told him that she was more worried about him than she was about herself. The thought made his stomach drop. He wanted to be there for her. He wanted to protect her and learning that he really couldn't was a hard pill to swallow. "Are you?"

"Yeah. Suspension won't deter them." She wrapped her arms around the books, clutching them to her chest until her knuckles turned white. "Fear of retribution might slow them down, but I wouldn't count on that either. Smashing Bryce's hand should've convinced them to back off. I don't want to spend my life in fear, but I don't want to be careless either." She paused for a few seconds and stared down at her feet. "I don't want you to get hurt again. I can't handle it."

There it was. The truth that he'd expected, but it hit him harder than he thought it would. "Don't worry about me." His arms hung at his sides, and his mouth tasted sour. He'd let her down, the one person he'd hoped he never would. He shook his head disgusted by himself.

"You don't understand, Cody." She clenched her fists and looked away from him. "I wanted to tear them apart. I wanted them to beg for mercy. That's why the water almost boiled. If I wouldn't have been so worried about you, I don't know what would've happened."

Her confession pulled him out of his thoughts. Maybe she didn't need him to be her sword. Maybe she needed him to be her shield. "I'm okay." He stroked her cheek with the back of his hand. "If I get hurt again, you'll heal me."

"Not necessarily." She kicked, sending several rocks scattering down the sidewalk. "One of these days, I'm going to fight a demon, and I might not walk away from that battle."

"That happens, isn't much hope for the rest of us." He grabbed her hand, and they started walking again. "Don't wanna be reckless, but wanna enjoy some time alone with you."

She sighed and nodded. "Let's just watch our backs."

"We make a good team. I get their attention while you take care of them." He threw a couple of quick punches. "Just need to come back before dark."

Sitting by the lake with his arm wrapped around Dacia's shoulders, he felt at peace. Ever since Alvin swung that bat at his knee, hatred had been building up inside of him. It wasn't gone, but it wasn't active either.

He watched the gentle lapping of water against the rocky shore and wondered why he hadn't asked Dacia out sooner. He'd wanted to take her to homecoming and to prom, but he'd chosen girls that didn't matter to him instead. How much better would those nights have been if he'd been brave enough to ask Dacia? Would she have said yes back then, or was being attacked the catalyst they needed to start a relationship?

She looked up at him. Her face blanched, and her breath caught. She stumbled to her feet, backing away, staring at him as if he was a ghost.

"What's wrong?" Cody jumped up, reaching for her.

She kept moving. Her eyes were wild, and her body trembled.

"Dacia!" He had no idea what had caused her terror, no idea what she was thinking. "Snap out of it!"

"I'm sorry, Cody." She turned and sprinted toward the trail.

He ran after her, closing the gap.

She dropped to the ground, curling her body over her knees, covering her face with her hands.

He slipped one hand onto her waist and one onto her shoulder, hoping to soothe her. "Are you okay? Did I do something wrong?" He knelt on the ground next to her.

When she didn't answer, he lifted her into a sitting position and held her. "It's okay, Dacia," he whispered while combing his fingers through her hair.

"I'm … I'm, so, so sorry." She sniffled and wiped her eyes with the heels of her hands. "I'm sorry."

Tension tightened every muscle in his body, and he dropped his hand. "Quit. Saying. That!" Some of the anger that had been building up inside of him escaped. He took a deep breath and softened his voice. "Please … tell me what's going on. Let me know what you're going through, but don't keep apologizing."

She took a deep breath, and her bottom lip trembled like she was about to start crying. "Do you remember the night I woke up with my face covered in blood? Of course, you do. What a stupid question," she mumbled. "Anyway, that's how my dream started. We were sitting by Falcon Lake, nobody else around, just enjoying each other's company. I freaked out. I knew I would glance over at you and see Bryce sitting in your place. I just—" her words caught on a sob that she tried to hold in "—I just panicked."

He held her close and whispered in her ear, "Dacia, I'll always be here for you. I'd never hurt you."

"I know." She clutched the hair on the top of her head. "That's why I feel so bad."

"Don't. You're going through a lot. If I were in your shoes, I may've done the same. It was a scary night for all of us." He brushed his thumb along her cheek. The wildness in her eyes had receded, and instead of looking terrified, she looked fragile. "Can I kiss you now?"

She didn't answer, just lifted her mouth to his. Her lips were like velvet. They moved against his slowly at first. Soft and soothing.

He followed her lead. When she pressed her body against his, he pulled her onto his lap. His hands slid to the small of her back, and she wrapped her arms around his neck, effectively eliminating all the space between their bodies.

He pulled his lips from hers, releasing a ragged breath as he trailed kisses over her chin and along her neck to her collarbone. She nudged his head with her nose, and he crushed his mouth against hers. The kiss softened, and she laid her head on his shoulder, both of them breathing hard.

"We should go." He didn't want to. He wanted to stay here with her, like this, forever. He kissed her temple before drawing back. "It'll be dark soon."

He stood, pulled her to her feet, and dusted the gravel off of her knees. Then he strolled back to where they'd been sitting and retrieved Sarah's journals. By the lake, it wasn't dark yet, but on the trail, the trees blocked most of the light. He should have thought about that. He clutched her hand, praying nothing would happen on their journey.

Dacia lifted her other hand into the air, and a small ball of fire appeared in her palm.

Warmth spread through Cody's chest, and he stood a little taller for the rest of their walk back to campus.

Chapter 14

What Possessed You?

It wasn't quite time for Cody to leave to get Dacia, but since Drew was heading out, Cody walked with him to Wisteria Hall. Getting to know Sarah had made things easier on Cody. He didn't have to stand outside and wait for somebody to buzz him in. His student ID gave him access to this building as well as his own.

He jogged up the three flights of stairs and knocked lightly on her door. Dacia opened it, and he stepped in, swinging her into his arms. She gasped, and he chuckled, low and raspy.

"Missed you," he whispered right before he skimmed his lips across hers.

She slid her hands up his chest, sending tingles racing throughout his body, and wrapped her arms around his neck, pulling them closer together. The quick brush of his lips intensified, leaving them both breathing heavy.

"Ready for class?" He took one step back, needing to put some space between them.

She did the same, widening the gap. "I'm ready, but I don't want to go."

"Me either, but already missed two days—"

"—so another won't hurt."

Cody snickered. "More along the lines of … so we need to go today."

"I knew you'd say that. That's why I'm dressed, my hair is combed, and my teeth are brushed." She picked up her backpack, and as soon as they were in the hallway, Cody draped his arm over her shoulders.

His fingers brushed her neck, and he fiddled with the chain she was wearing. It was thick and heavy. "Noticed this yesterday. Where'd it come from?" He pulled it up so that he could see it better. "Looks ancient."

She swatted his hand, making him drop it. "Because it is. Sarah gave it to me to help protect me from Nefarious."

Some of the easy-going nature that he'd had since she opened the door disappeared. A demon. Could it be real? How would they know when it returned to Earth? How would it know to show up where Dacia was? Was there really even a chance that it was true? He shook off the depressing thoughts. He was here with Dacia, and he needed to enjoy it.

They were almost to the Quartz Building when the cat's eye started glowing blue. "Cody—" Dacia stopped and pointed at the amulet "—*look*."

Cody's mind raced. Nefarious? Here? In the middle of campus on a bright sunny morning. Why weren't people screaming or running for their lives? He spun in a circle, scanning the area for danger. He didn't see anything. "Why?" He stared at her, wondering If she had any insight.

She doubled over, clutching her stomach. Her breath was ragged. Cody rubbed her back, feeling her heart racing.

After a couple of minutes, she straightened, flipped her hair over her shoulder, and the two of them continued to class.

Cody glanced at her several times, wondering if she wanted to talk about it, but she just stared straight ahead, putting one foot in front of the other.

As they neared Quartz Building, Dacia gasped. "What are they doing here? They're supposed to be suspended."

Cody saw them, too. The Potato Heads stood by the doorway. His stomach tightened, and the magma burned inside of him again. He lifted his hand to Dacia's neck, massaging it, hoping to ease some of her tension. "Just breathe." He tried to keep the anger and hatred out of his voice.

"Don't you get it?" She poked him in the ribs, taking him completely off guard.

His hand slipped, and he sucked in a breath. "What?"

She pointed at them, then at the amulet. "They're here, and this is glowing."

Realization was a slap in Cody's face. His eyes widened, and his head jerked back. "So, they really are—"

"—under Nefarious' control." She staggered back as she said the words.

Cody narrowed his eyes and pulled himself up straighter. Then he held his hand out. "Come on, Dacia. They can't do anything here."

She stuffed the necklace under her shirt, and instead of taking his hand, she wrapped her arm around his waist, clutching his hoodie in her fist.

"Well, look who's here. It's the freak and gimpy," Alvin bellowed. "How ya feeling Cody?" The four of them laughed.

Cody tensed. He fought down the magma, refusing to let it erupt. Not here. Not now. When he spoke, his voice was steady. "Fine. Thanks for asking."

As they walked closer, one by one the Potato Heads' laughter died. They looked at Cody with drawn eyebrows and tilted heads. Their mouths hung open. They glanced at each other as if wondering if they were all seeing the same thing.

"You don't even have a bruise." Bryce rubbed his hand over his mouth.

"I … I don't understand." Cassandra slumped as if she'd been deflated. "You shouldn't even be out of the hospital yet."

Cody wanted to lash out at them. He wanted to attack, to show them that he wasn't just a target that they could aim at whenever they got the notion, but that wasn't the answer. "I'm a quick healer." Hoping he could pull off a nonchalant attitude, he shrugged one shoulder. "Don't you have a hearing to attend?" He didn't spare them a glance as he pressed his hand against the small of Dacia's back and led her to the doors.

The desire to look over his shoulder and make sure they weren't following him was nearly overwhelming, but through the grace of God, he was able to keep his eyes forward and his steps steady.

As soon as they were inside, Dacia let out the breath she'd been holding. "How did you handle that so well?" She let go of his sweatshirt, smoothing it down afterward. Her touch was a soothing balm. "They weren't even talking to me, and I wanted to punch them. It has to be eating at you."

"They're not worth it. They'll never change." He looked over his shoulder toward the door and shook his head. They hadn't come inside. Maybe his bluff had worked. He squeezed her fingers, wondering what she would think if she knew about the hatred that had taken root inside of him. "Think I'm afraid of 'em, they'll keep coming. Think they're not bothering me, maybe they'll back off."

She sat at her desk, overlooking the stage where she'd stood when she caught Cassandra's books on fire. "I guess that's a good way to look at it, but if they're possessed, they won't stop until this is over."

"Can't give up." Cody picked up her hand and brought it to his lips, pressing a kiss to the soft skin. "Be careful." He strode toward the door and sucked in a deep breath, hoping he looked confident to her because he felt anything but. Bryce and his friends weren't about to give up. They wouldn't make this easy, and if they were possessed by Nefarious, things were going to get much worse before they got better.

"Cody—" Dacia ran up behind him and grabbed his arm, jerking him to a stop "—go out the back door."

Relief flooded him. He didn't know why he hadn't thought about it. He tipped his head forward slightly. "Do. Not. Leave. Without. Me."

Cody wondered if the downpour was Dacia's doing or if it was a natural storm. When he started walking to Sarah's office, it had been raining, but nothing horrible. Not long after though, the rain started coming down in sheets. It rushed down the sidewalk and pooled in the lawn.

When he arrived at Cacomistle Hall, he didn't want to go in. He didn't want to drip all over the hardwood floor and staircase, but he didn't have a choice. His phone didn't work here, and Dacia, he hoped, wouldn't leave without him.

He walked up and knocked on the door, opening it, but refusing to step inside Sarah's office. He didn't need to drip on her carpet, too. "Dacia, you ready?"

She flung her jacket over her shoulders and slipped her arms through the sleeves. "As ready as I'll ever be."

"Do you want an umbrella?" Sarah stood and started walking toward her office.

"No, won't hold up in this wind." Cody shivered. "It's brutal."

She pointed at the flames, dancing in the fireplace. "Would you like to come in and get warmed up?"

"No." His teeth chattered, and he shivered uncontrollably. "I'd like to get dry clothes on. I'm freezing."

"Have a good weekend, Sarah." Dacia strode over and slid her hand into Cody's.

"You too, Dacia … be careful."

They walked down the stairs. Lightning flashed through the windows, lighting up the night sky. They stood in the entryway, and Cody squeezed her hand. "Rain's freezing." He pushed the door open, letting Dacia go through.

The torrent pelted down all around, but not even a single drop landed on them. Cody looked up to see why. They seemed to be inside a giant invisible bubble. "Cool." Rain pummeled the enclosure. He marveled at this new power. Could she do anything she set her mind to, or were there limits?

"Coulda used this on the way to get ya." He lifted his arm to drape it over her shoulder, but she dodged.

Smiling at him, she shook her head. "You're soaked."

"And you should be." He laughed, and while she wasn't expecting it, he grabbed her around the waist and pulled her back so that she was flush against his body.

She giggled and clung to him. "Do you want to go to your room to get some dry clothes?"

"Nah, I dropped some off." He reached his hand out, and the bubble extended. "You're the best umbrella ever."

Dacia darted ahead, but Cody caught up quickly, wrapping her in his arms and dragging her back. He rested his head on top of her curls and practically waddled with his feet on the outside of hers. "You're not getting away that easily." He soundlessly chuckled.

Without ever letting go, he stepped beside her. She laid her head against his arm. If he wasn't freezing, he would have drawn out the walk. Moments like these were precious, but as soon as another shiver wracked his body, she picked up her pace.

"Jeez, Cody." Samantha sat at the computer with books and notepads spread out all over the desk. "How did you get soaked? Dacia's hardly wet at all."

"I used him as an umbrella." Dacia laughed while flexing her arm muscles.

"Unfortunately, Dacia wasn't with me on the way." He hung his jacket on the hook by the door, grabbed the duffel with his spare clothes in it, and left the room to change.

Cody ran down the stairs to the public restrooms. He was frozen to his core. Rivulets ran off his hair and onto his sweatshirt. He grabbed a towel out of his bag and dried off before changing into dry blue jeans and a blue sweater that Dacia had always liked. Before they were dating, she had told him that it made his eyes look bluer. He hurried back to her room and knocked on the door.

"Looking good." Dacia wiggled her eyebrows at him when she let him in.

As soon as he closed the door, she stood on her toes, wrapped her arms around his neck, and pulled his mouth down on hers.

He dropped his bag on the floor and splayed his hands over her back, returning her kiss with fervor.

"This is not the time for kissing." Samantha smacked the table. "Dacia just showed me what she can do. It's amazing."

Cody leaned his forehead against Dacia's, calming his breath for a minute before wrapping his arm around her shoulders and leading her to Cookie Monster. He sat, then pulled her down on his lap. Holding her like this felt like the most natural thing in the world. Her body fit perfectly against his. "You weren't too tired?"

"No." She shook her head. "I'm going to have to figure out my limitations."

"But first dinner." Cody's stomach growled loud enough to let them know that he really was starving.

After walking through the downpour, Cody wasn't willing to go back out again. They called the pizza place for delivery. He felt a little sorry for whoever had to bring it to them but not bad enough to get it himself.

"Why you going home?" Cody asked Samantha, thinking that talking about something other than Dacia's powers, the demon threat, or the Potato Heads might be a nice change.

"I haven't been home for a while." She set her pen on the desk and rolled her chair back. "Mom called me yesterday and asked if I remember where I live, so I decided I should go visit them."

"Since I started college, my parents have turned into quite the social butterflies." Dacia fiddled with the cuff of Cody's sweater.

Cody suddenly felt weighed down by life. He looked at his hand on Dacia's leg, staring at it until it blurred. "Glad Sarah couldn't get holda mine."

"You didn't call them?" Dacia tipped his chin up.

"I did, but couldn't tell them the truth." He wiped his hand down his face. He hated lying. Too often the truth came out when you weren't expecting it to. "Told 'em I had a kidney stone."

"Won't they figure it out when they get the bill?" Samantha asked.

"Nah. The hospital'll bill Phlox."

A knock ended their conversation. Cody stood up and set Dacia on her feet. He pulled his wallet out on his way to the door. When he carried the pizza to the desk, he let go of his somber feelings. He wanted an evening without worries.

They ate and played video games, and at midnight, Marcy showed up to kick Cody out for the night.

He pulled Dacia to her feet, sliding his hands up her neck. She shivered in response to his touch. That he could have that effect on her filled him with a sense of satisfaction. He tipped her head back and pressed his lips against hers.

She clutched his sweater in both hands, pulling him closer. "Don't leave," she whispered.

"Have to. Marcy won't go away 'til I do." His lips brushed over hers again, and he wanted to stay more than anything. "Good night. Sleep tight." He forced himself to walk through the door.

Chapter 15

Sneaking Out

The phone rang, waking Cody from a fitful sleep. He jumped out of his loft and answered on the second ring. "Hello." His voice was thick.

"Another nightmare," Samantha said without so much as a hello. "She's hurt again."

Suddenly, he was wide awake. He grabbed the sweats off his ladder and tugged them on. "Be there in a few."

"Booty call?" Drew peered over his railing, wagging his eyebrows at Cody.

Cody shook his head. He didn't have time for this right now. "Dacia's hurt." He shoved his feet into his shoes and ran through the dorm and out into the night.

Samantha must have been watching through the peephole because as soon as Cody arrived, the door opened, and she ushered him in. "I'm going back to sleep. Try to keep it down, okay?"

"How bad?" Cody's heart squeezed when he asked.

She climbed into her loft, tucked her arm under her pillow, and looked down at him. "She wouldn't say." She yawned. "Goodnight."

"Goodnight, Sam." Cody turned and watched for Dacia to come back. "And thanks."

The clock stopped moving, but Cody felt every agonizing second stretch into hours. He couldn't stand still any longer. He dragged his hands down his face and started pacing. *What's taking her so long anyway?* He debated going in search of her, but he didn't want to get caught in the halls after hours again.

He was across the room when he heard the knob turn.

Dacia stepped in and immediately spun toward the door. She leaned against it as she checked the lock. "Get a grip."

He wouldn't have heard her if he'd been more than a couple of steps away. He moved closer and wrapped his arms around her waist. "If you want me to."

She spun around with her hand pressed to her chest. Her eyes were opened wide, the whites of them showing all around her irises. "Don't ever do that again!"

He fought to hide his smile. "Sorry." He looked from her face to her arm, and his expression turned serious. Samantha told him that Dacia had woken with a burnt arm, but he hadn't expected it to look charred. Besides the burn, there was a small cut on her chin. He looked her over, wondering if she was injured anywhere else. "You okay?"

"A little spooked." She nodded at her arm, not allowing her gaze to linger on it for too long, and shuddered. "I can't feel that yet. I hope it heals before I can."

"Spooked?" He hadn't expected that. He figured she would say sore or freaked out or something along those lines.

She nodded. "What are you doing here anyway?"

"Samantha thought you might wander off, so she called me."

Dacia glanced up at Samantha's loft. She was either sleeping or pretending to.

"I'm going to sleep in Cookie Monster … unless you want to talk." He raised his eyebrow in a challenge. "Actually"—he rubbed his jaw, not sure how she would handle what he was about to divulge—"plan to sleep in one of these 'til this is over."

"You can't stay here! What about Marcy?"

He pressed his finger to her lips and leaned in close to her face. "Quiet, and she'll never know."

A strange look crossed her face as she stared at him, and he couldn't help but wonder what she was thinking.

"It's one o'clock." His gaze slipped to her arm. How could something like that happen? He'd peeked at her bed while he was waiting for her to come back. The sheets were fine. There was no evidence of a fire. Her pillowcase had some blood on it, but he'd changed that for her. Looking into her green eyes, he said, "If she knew I came in, she'd've kicked me out."

"Fine." She took a step back. "I'm going to bed."

He closed the distance and pulled her close to him. He brushed the hair off of her face, tucking it behind her ear. Then he kissed her before sitting in the chair.

Something woke Cody up. It took him a few seconds to remember why he was sleeping in the chair in Dacia's room, but as soon as he did, he looked up into her loft. Not seeing her, he jumped to his feet, walked over, and climbed the first two rungs of her ladder.

Glacier, her white teddy bear, was twisted in the blankets, but Dacia was gone.

"Sam." Cody fought to keep his voice down as panic surged inside of him. "Know where Dacia went?" he asked when she looked at him.

Her eyes rolled back, and he thought she was going to fall back to sleep. Instead, she lifted onto her elbows. "She's gone?"

His legs trembled. He fell off the ladder, stumbling until his knees hit the chair. He plopped down hard. "Where would she go?"

"I'll go check the restroom." Samantha walked over to the door, holding onto the handle. "Maybe she had to pee."

While she was gone, Cody paced. He rubbed the back of his neck, trying to calm his nerves, but something was wrong. He could feel it. If she was just going to the restroom, she would have told him. She wouldn't have needed to sneak out.

"She's not there." The door snicked shut behind Samantha.

Cody put his shoes on. While he tied them, he said, "I'm going looking for her."

"I'll go with you."

They walked quietly through the halls, hoping to remain unnoticed. When they stepped outside, they were enveloped by a dense fog. The glow from the streetlights did nothing to cut through it. There was no way they would find Dacia out here unless they just happened to stumble upon her.

"Why would she come outside in this?" Samantha's eyes were wide, and she wrapped her jacket around her as if it could somehow protect her.

Cody turned around, looking for anything that might lead him to Dacia. "Don't know." He dragged his hand down his face and started walking toward the road. "What was she thinking?"

Samantha stayed right next to him. Her gaze darted from side to side, and a couple of times, she grabbed hold of his arm. "Sorry." She pulled her hand away, waving it through the fog. "It's creepy out here tonight."

They covered the main part of campus. "Guess we go back." Cody sighed. "She might be there again."

"She'll be okay." Samantha's hand rested on his shoulder. This time it wasn't fear that drove her to touch him.

They hurried through the halls, moving as quietly as possible. Cody held his breath while Samantha unlocked the door. He pinched his eyes shut as she swung it open.

The room was empty.

He trudged over to Cookie Monster, sank into the chair, and clutched its arms. All he could do now was hope and pray.

Time slowed to a crawl. Cody pictured Dacia lying somewhere broken and bleeding. He imagined her fighting a demon.

He thought about what the Potato Heads had done to him when they caught him off guard and wondered if they'd done the same to her.

His stomach tightened, and he thought he might throw up. He looked at the clock for the hundredth time in the last few minutes.

The phone rang, and Cody practically pounced on it. "H-hello." His voice was too loud.

Samantha put her finger over her lips and glanced at the door.

"Cody, what's wrong?" Dacia asked.

How could she ask him what was wrong? Didn't she realize what waking up and finding her gone would do to him? "Where are you?" He didn't wait for an answer. "Are you okay?"

"I'm fine." She wasn't, though. There was something in her voice that Cody couldn't make out.

"Woke up and you were gone. Why?" Desperation clung to his voice. "Samantha and I looked, but in this fog, can't see anything. Where are you?"

"I'm in Sarah's office." There was a slight pause between each word. "I need sleep. I'll tell you and Sam—" she yawned "—all about it over breakfast."

"Be there in a few," Cody said and hung up.

The phone rang almost as soon as he set the receiver in its cradle. He looked at Samantha and shook his head. "She's in Sarah's office. Doesn't want us to come."

"Too bad." Samantha pulled her hoodie on and waited by the door. "Let's go."

Knowing that the fog creeped her out, Cody held Samantha's hand as they raced to Cacomistle Hall.

Sarah opened the door for them. Her face was pale, and it looked like it was a struggle for her to keep her eyes open.

"Where's Dacia?" Cody asked.

Sarah pointed at the floor. "She collapsed."

Cody strode over and knelt next to her. Her arm was no longer charred. The skin was red and blistered. He lifted her, careful not to touch her burn, carried her to the couch, and laid her on it. She didn't move at all.

"What happened?" Samantha glared down at Dacia before focusing on Sarah.

Sarah shook her head and lay on the other sofa. Her eyes closed almost immediately. "Tomorrow," she answered before drifting off to sleep.

Cody sat on the floor in front of Dacia, propped his arm on the cushion, and rested his head on it. "Get some rest."

Samantha folded her arms over her chest and shook her head. "This is ridiculous." She sat at the end of the couch Dacia was on and put her feet on the coffee table. "I should've stayed in my warm bed. It's more comfortable and has blankets."

Cody nodded. He couldn't disagree with her, but he was glad to be there where, hopefully, he would know if Dacia left again.

"What do you suppose happened?" Samantha asked, snapping him out of his thoughts.

He looked at Dacia and Sarah both sleeping like the dead and shook his head. "Something." Dacia had slept like this that day that she had exhausted her powers. Something must have taken a toll on her, but he didn't want to think about what that might be. "They're both outta it."

When Samantha didn't say anything else, he closed his eyes, drifting off to the sound of Dacia's steady breaths next to his ear.

Dacia stirred, and Cody sat up. This time, he wasn't about to let her go.

"Morning, sleepyhead," Cody said while she stretched like a cat.

"Hey." She sat up and combed her fingers through her hair. "When did you get here?"

Cody turned on the floor so that he was looking at her. "Five minutes after your call."

"Thanks for waiting up for us," Samantha snipped.

"I'm sorry." Dacia dropped her gaze. "I collapsed."

"We could've used some sleep." Samantha looked like she hadn't gotten any rest in the last week or so. Her brown eyes were rimmed in red, and heavy bags sat beneath them. "But between your nightmares and sneaking off, we didn't get much rest."

"I'm sorry." Dacia twisted the strings on her hoodie together until they were pressed against her neck. Then she straightened them out and did it over again. "I couldn't help it. I literally collapsed."

"Explains you lying on the floor." Cody had wondered about that when they came in last night, but Sarah had fallen asleep before he could ask.

There was a long pause where Dacia stared out the window at the mountains. Cody followed her gaze. The fog had cleared sometime during the night, leaving the sky a crisp, clear blue.

"Did either of you get any sleep?" she asked.

"With my head right here"—Cody patted the couch—"so I'd know if you moved."

"I tried to sleep at the end of the couch." Samantha didn't sound quite so annoyed. "Here—" she tossed Dacia the necklace "—you left this hanging on your bed."

Dacia turned the amulet over, looking at it like it might have some answers for her. Then she glanced around the room. "Where's Sarah?"

"Went to get breakfast." Cody moved up onto the couch and wrapped his arm around Dacia's shoulders, pulling her against his side.

"Did she tell you about last night?" Dacia's voice shrank with each word.

"No. When we got here, she could barely keep her eyes open. Her face was really pale. She looked sick." Samantha paced the room, stopping with her hands on her hips. "I want to know what would make you consider going out on your own in the middle of the night after what happened last time."

"That uneasy feeling I've had lately made me get out of bed. I knew I had to leave the room, and I knew you two would try to talk me out of it." She shivered, and Cody rubbed her arm, trying to warm her up and soothe her at the same time. "I didn't want to go out on my own. Believe me, I was scared to death, but it was something I *had* to do. And I had to do it immediately."

"Breakfast is here," Sarah announced as she stepped through the door. "Dacia, I see you finally woke up."

She shot Samantha a sidelong glance, then focused on Sarah. "Yeah, I actually slept pretty well after passing out."

"That's good to hear. Cody, would you mind clearing the coffee table? We'll eat there." Sarah kicked her shoes off, then walked over to them, placing donuts, coffee, and milk on the table. Looking at Samantha, she said, "Why don't you have a seat, and we'll talk about last night. I want to start with Dacia's dream."

Dacia didn't grab any food, didn't wait for Samantha to sit, didn't hesitate. "I saw Nefarious."

"In your dream?" Cody asked.

"Yes."

Samantha held her donut in the air in front of her mouth. "What was he like?"

Dacia stared straight ahead, but Cody didn't think she was seeing anything in the room with them. Suddenly, she gasped for air.

He patted her on the back, looking helplessly from her to Sarah.

"Dacia"—Sarah's voice was calm, soothing—"relax. I want you to find yourself in front of the mountain lake. Picture yourself sitting there, staring out at the tranquil reflection. Feel the cool mountain breeze blow through your hair."

Cody watched Dacia. She closed her eyes. After several minutes, her muscles relaxed, and she leaned into him more. Her breathing slowly returned to normal.

When she opened her eyes, Samantha asked, "Are you okay, Dacia?"

"Yeah, for now." She rested her elbows on her knees and stared down at her hands while describing Nefarious. "He was massive." She shuddered. "He had horns and fangs and claws and a whip and a sword. Wings and a spiked tail." She looked up for just an instant. "So many weapons to use against me, and I have what?" Without waiting for an answer, she went on. "When I was in his presence, I felt pure evil and hatred. Thoughts raced through my mind." She paused and rubbed the palm of her hand with her thumb. "No, not thoughts, suggestions. When I turned and saw him, all hope fled. There's no way I can defeat him. He's more evil … more monstrous than I ever imagined he would be."

Cody lifted her onto his lap, needing to comfort her. "Don't give up yet."

"It's too late." That was the only acknowledgment she gave him before delving into her dream. "I don't know how I got this cut." She rubbed the bottom of her chin. "My nightmare started with Nefarious standing over me. I was defeated. There was no hope." She clutched Cody's hand. "But Cody was out there. He was calling my name, and I was afraid Nefarious would go after him, so I got up.

"I shot lightning bolts at him, but he absorbed them." Tears rimmed her eyes, but they didn't fall. "His whip flew through the air at me, only singeing my shoes. Then he let it fly again. This time—" her eyes darted toward Cody "—it wrapped around you. I … I was too late."

"It's okay, Dacia." Cody rubbed his hand down her arm, then back up. "I'm here. I'm okay."

She looked up at him, and a half-hearted smile touched her lips. "He threw a fireball at me, and I tried to block it with ice, but it wasn't enough. When Samantha woke me up, my chin was bleeding, and my arm was burned beyond recognition." She lifted one shoulder toward her ear like it was no big deal, but she wasn't fooling anyone.

Sarah nodded like this all made perfect sense. "Let's move on to the rest of the night's events from Dacia's perspective. How did you find me?"

"For the last couple of days, I've known something bad was going to happen."

"We know." Samantha's leg tapped against the ground in a staccato beat.

Dacia rubbed the arm that had been burned last night, then spoke so softly that Cody wondered if Sarah could hear her. "I woke up. My arm was healing, and the pain was horrific. I climbed out of bed and thought about waking you guys, but I knew I needed to leave, and I didn't have time to debate it." Her shoulders curled over her body, and her chin quivered. "I raced down the stairs and outside. I almost went back when I saw how foggy it was. It was super creepy being out there by myself."

Cody remembered his fear from last night. Most of it was brought on by Dacia's absence, but now that he knew mystical creatures existed, some of it could have been attributed to the fog and what could have been hiding in it.

"I heard somebody scream and ran toward it. When I got there, Sarah's body was lying on the ground." Dacia sucked in a deep breath and stared straight ahead. "She wasn't breathing."

Samantha gasped, but Dacia didn't seem to notice. She just continued reciting her story. "Nefarious kept telling me to leave. To give up. That I couldn't save her." She looked Sarah in the eyes. "I almost left you so many times."

Sarah nodded. "It couldn't have been easy."

If Dacia heard what Sarah said, she didn't acknowledge it.

"She gasped for breath, and I kept pushing my power into her until she wasn't struggling so much." Dacia rolled one of her hoodie strings up, then let it go. "I helped her up, levitated her, and we rushed back here. I had enough energy to call you before I passed out. " She grabbed hold of Cody's hand. "What were you doing out alone at that time of night?" she asked Sarah.

"You sound like my mother." Sarah laughed. "Nancy Heron called and told me Cassandra was hurt. I went out to check on her. The fog was awful. I couldn't see at all."

"Yeah, we went out to look for Dacia," Samantha said with a shiver.

Cody cleared his throat. "You think Nefarious brought the fog?"

Sarah covered her mouth with a finger while rubbing her chin. "It's a definite possibility."

"It kept him hidden." Dacia nodded. "You left to check on Cassandra. Then what?"

"Suddenly, in front of me, I saw the yellow eyes that Dacia's described so many times. I keep rewinding the events in my mind, but I don't know what happened. One minute I stared into those eyes. The next, I was lying face down on the ground. The air was torn from my lungs, and everything faded into nothingness. I heard laughter in my mind. It was strange … like a thought. Around me was silence, but in my head was this laughter followed by a voice telling me Dacia would be next, that she couldn't survive without her mentor. Then he said, 'The world will, at last, be mine.' There was more laughter, then nothing. I think I died."

Samantha's hand shot up to her chest. "Oh, my God."

Dacia snuggled into Cody, and he held her tighter, rubbing her arm.

"The next thing I remember Dacia told me we had to get out of there. We came back here, and Dacia collapsed."

After a few seconds, Dacia asked, "Have you talked to Nancy?"

"Yes, I called her last night after you fell asleep and told her I would come by in the morning because of the fog. So, I went there before getting breakfast."

"We wondered what was taking so long," Samantha said.

"Cassandra had to have several stitches in her leg, but she'll be fine." Sarah took a drink of her coffee, then pulled the lid off and dumped a container of creamer into it. "She wouldn't tell Nancy what happened to her."

Dacia tucked her hands into her hoodie's pouch. "My guess is Nefarious used her as a pawn to get you out in the open."

"Yeah, I thought about that." Sarah rubbed her hands down her legs. "But there's no way to prove it."

"You were killed by a demon." Cody looked directly into Sarah's hazel eyes, wondering why he didn't see any fear there, wondering how she could be sitting across from them so calmly. "Why aren't you scared to death?"

"I faced evil and walked away from it. What else is there to be afraid of?"

Chapter 16

Cody drove to Althea. Dacia rode next to him. Her hand rested on his thigh as he navigated the curvy road. Samantha was in the backseat. When she had first gotten in, he thought it was a good thing she was short. He didn't think he would be able to fit back there.

Nobody said much on the ride. He didn't know about them, but he was still replaying the conversations from that morning. Somehow, if Sarah was right and she'd been dead, Dacia had brought her back to life. Her powers were growing rapidly, and they were a bit scary. If she could give a life just by touching someone and pushing her power into them, could she take a life that easily? At what point would her powers stop growing?

When he drove past the place where she'd wrecked her truck, he took her hand in his, gently squeezing her fingers. He smiled at her, hoping she knew that he knew how hard this was on her and that he just couldn't quite put it into words.

With no real destination in mind, somehow, they ended up at Mountain View Putt-Putt. Cody and Dacia had played miniature golf together on several occasions but never here. They walked up to the counter, paid their fees, picked out a ball and a club, then walked through the office's backdoor and onto the course. Flagstone walkways meandered through beds filled with wildflowers and boulders. There were waterfalls and ponds next to most holes. The "greens" were a tan color that blended well with the overall design.

The game gave him something other than Nefarious and his growing fear for Dacia's life to focus on. He concentrated on sinking his putt. Then he laughed as Dacia took six or seven tries to get her ball into the hole. Samantha did a little better but nowhere near as good as him.

By the sixteenth hole, Cody thought he might keel over if they didn't get lunch soon. "You wanna go to The Avalanche?"

"Sure," Samantha said. "It should only take Dacia an hour or so to finish up."

Dacia tried to give her a stern look, but her lips kept curling into a smile. "Laugh all you want, but I'm perfecting my stance. If I hit it in on the first try, I wouldn't get near as much practice."

Without the distraction of hitting the ball, lunch was fairly quiet. They all seemed to fall back into their thoughts again.

Dacia stared down at her pasta. "I need to quit dwelling on this," she mumbled.

Cody and Samantha both looked over at her. When she didn't say anything else, he realized she was talking to herself. "Just don't argue with yourself." Cody shoved a handful of fries into his mouth.

"Actually"—Samantha pointed her fork at him—"you don't have to worry about her until she loses an argument with herself."

Cody watched Dacia push the food around on her plate. The chicken Alfredo had to be getting cold, but she hadn't even taken a single bite yet. He placed his hand on top of hers. She glanced down at it, then into his eyes.

"You need to eat." He rubbed his thumb over her wrist.

She nodded, looking at her food, then looking away with her lip curled up. "I know, but I can't."

Cody finished his burger without saying anything else to Dacia about eating. When the waitress came by with their check, he asked her for a box for Dacia's untouched lunch. "Now what?" he asked.

"I, uh, think I'm ready to go back." Samantha looked around nervously. "I'm a little on edge."

"Back to campus, it is then." Cody grabbed Dacia's leftovers as he stood, then he slid his other hand over hers, twining their fingers together while they walked to the car. He unlocked the passenger door first and waited while Samantha and Dacia got in. Then he walked to his side.

Driving back to campus, he tapped his thumb against the steering wheel. Dacia hadn't said a word since leaving The Avalanche, and he was worried about her. He glanced over surreptitiously, but he needn't have bothered. Her shoulders were slumped, and she stared out the side window. He wondered if she was seeing anything at all or if she was stuck in her head in some memory or vision. Deciding she wasn't capable of a confrontation, he drove up to the front door of the women's dorms and dropped Samantha and Dacia off. Normally, she would've argued, but she was lost somewhere in her thoughts. He parked, then walked them to their room. He pulled the door shut behind him but didn't move away from it. "You okay?" he asked softly.

She nodded, but he could see the truth. She was scared. He cupped her cheek, brushing his thumb under her eye. "Gotta go for a bit, but I'll be back."

"Please be careful, and call me when you get there." She grabbed his hand.

"I will." He pulled her closer, holding her face in his hands, breathing in her vanilla and roses scent. "I'll be fine."

She hooked her fingers in his belt loops. "Don't go."

His knees buckled, and his heart gave a painful squeeze. He felt like a dog that had been commanded to sit. He wanted to do it, to make her happy, to stay with her, and never let her out of his sight, but he needed to take a shower and grab extra clothes. Whether she wanted him to or not, he had every intention of sleeping in Cookie Monster again tonight.

Looking into her emerald eyes, he dropped his hands to her shoulders, then trailed them down her arms, finally coming to a rest at her waist.

She twined her arms around his neck and pulled his mouth down. As Cody's lips moved against hers, he became increasingly aware of the heat of her soft body pressed against his. He curled his hand into her hair and pressed her closer to him.

She was his, and he was hers.

Her mouth moved against his with a fervor he'd never felt from her before, making him realize just how scared she was. Eventually, she slowed the kiss, and he pulled away. He rested his forehead against hers, not quite ready to let go. "Be back before you know it."

She kissed him once more, just a swipe of her lips over his.

Knowing how nervous Dacia was, Cody jogged to his room. A few minutes after leaving hers, he called. "Made it," he said when she answered the phone. "See you in a bit, okay?"

"Yeah, thanks for calling."

"No problem. I love you, Dacia." The words slipped out without him giving them any thought. She already had to know he loved her, didn't she? "Please, don't leave."

"I love you, too." Life returned to her voice. In fact, she sounded almost giddy.

He smiled at the phone as he placed it in its cradle. Then he worked on a few homework assignments, rushing through them more than he normally would. Even still, they took him over two hours to complete. As soon as he finished, he grabbed his clothes and bathroom bag and headed to the showers. He didn't normally shave every day, but he stood in front of the mirror and spent extra time on it. He wanted his face to be smooth so that if Dacia kissed him like she had earlier, the tiny hairs around his mouth wouldn't scratch her.

By the time he was ready to go back to Dacia's dorm, nearly three hours had passed. He hadn't planned on being gone for that long, so he hurried, hoping he hadn't caused her any undue stress.

He knocked on her door, but nobody answered. He stood there staring at it, wondering what could have happened that would make both of them leave. Had they decided to take showers now instead of waiting until later tonight? Had something happened to Sarah again? Had Dacia fallen asleep and gotten injured?

He pounded on the door, hoping that Dacia had fallen asleep or was concentrating on something and just hadn't heard him the first time. When nobody answered again, his stomach churned.

He folded his arms and stood in front of her door. His thoughts raced in a thousand directions, always coming up with horrible possibilities and even worse outcomes.

Then he heard her and Samantha walking down the hall. Dacia's hair was windblown, her cheeks rosy. Normally, he would have thought it was cute but not now. He fisted his hands at his sides. The veins in his arms stood over the top of his flexed muscles. "Thought we had an understanding." Cody forced the words out through clenched teeth.

"I didn't go anywhere on my own." She used both hands to draw his attention to Samantha.

Samantha stopped in front of him, looking at him for a second before saying, "Let me in, Cody." She put her hand on his arm, and his posture loosened fractionally.

"Where. Have. You. Been?" His pulse was racing, and heat spread through his body. He ground his teeth together.

"Not here." She pointed at the open doors lining the hallway.

He stepped to the side, and Samantha unlocked the door. "Come on in."

Once they were inside, he turned toward Dacia. Controlling his temper a little better, he asked, "What happened?"

Dacia cleared her throat and looked at Samantha as if trying to figure out what to say. "I just had an … uh, interesting chat with Bryce."

His chest heaved, and his nostrils flared. He didn't want to yell at her, but he couldn't conceal the venom that filled his voice. "What'd the little weasel want?"

"He said that Cassandra is in a trance." She paced between the chairs. "He said that she had dreams about me before college started, and she knew I would try to hurt them."

Cody wiped his hand down his face. "Explains a lot."

"He said they know what I'm trying to do." She stopped right in front of him. "All I wanted was to live a normal life. I didn't want more people to find out about my powers." She leaned her head against his chest.

He put his hand on her back and tried to relax a little bit. "And he let you walk away? He didn't try to hurt you?"

"Actually"—Samantha sat in the desk chair and spun it from side to side—"Bryce walked away. We waited to leave until he was gone."

Dacia staggered back from Cody, hitting her hip against the wall.

"Dacia—" Cody grabbed her hand "—tell me what you're thinking." He wasn't sure what was going on.

"I, uh …" She pulled her hand through her hair and slid down the wall to the floor.

Cody looked over at Samantha, but she just shook her head in response to his unasked question. He turned back toward Dacia, then knelt in front of her. He felt the anger drain out of him.

She placed her hand on his cheek, and he leaned into her touch.

"Please, Dacia," he murmured.

She closed her eyes. "What if I did it?"

"Did what?" He blinked at her several times, trying to make sense of what she was saying.

Shaking her head, she said, "Put Cassandra in a coma."

Samantha snorted before saying, "Then you should do it to the other three, so they leave you alone until this is over."

"Sounds reasonable." Cody agreed completely, but he knew Dacia would see it differently. He knew how much her powers weighed on her.

"There's just one thing I don't understand," Samantha said.

"What?" Cody asked.

"Cassandra went to Nancy Heron last night because she cut her leg. If she's in a trance or whatever, how did she get there? And, how did she get hurt in the first place?"

Dacia wrapped her arms around her legs and rocked back and forth. "I wondered that, but I didn't want to be the one to tell Bryce she'd been out." She pushed her hands against the ground and stood up. "What I'd like to know is why the amulet didn't heat up when Bryce came over."

"It can't be a coincidence that it did before," Samantha said.

"No." She fiddled with the heavy chain of the necklace. "But all four of them were there that day."

Dacia set her hand on Cody's arm, and he jerked awake.

"You okay?" His voice came out gravelly and rough with sleep, but he was alert.

"Fine." She combed her fingers through her hair, trying to tame her wild curls. "I can't sleep. I'm going to walk the hallway and see if I can clear my head."

He reached for his shoes but stopped with his hand in midair. "Can't go with you." He rubbed his face, then looked up at her, focusing on the freckles on the bridge of her nose. He'd always like that she didn't cover them with make-up. They made her look real, endearing. He tried to come up with a way to keep her here, but nothing he could say would make her stay. He sucked in a deep breath. "Promise you'll be careful."

She knelt in front of him, setting her hands on his knees. He leaned his forehead against hers, willing her to stay safe.

She closed her eyes and whispered, "I promise."

He brushed his thumb over her mouth. He couldn't force her to stay, but he could try to convince her. He leaned forward, capturing her lips with his. He'd never thought of himself as a thief, but he stole her breath. She wrapped her arms around his neck, pulling their bodies closer together.

His hands shook, so he gripped her tighter, never wanting to let go.

She pulled back, ending the kiss with a tender, sweet promise.

He held onto her hand as she stood. He felt the tension in his muscles increase as he fought the desire to pull her back, to keep her with him.

He let her pull him to his feet and walked with her to the door. "Fifteen minutes." His voice was rough. Whether from their kiss or barely clinging to his self-control, he wasn't sure. "After that, coming after you. Don't care if I get caught."

Her only response was a squeeze of his hand.

"Clock's ticking."

Fifteen minutes came and went. Cody stared up into Samantha's loft, wondering if he should wake her or just head out on his own. He stepped into his shoes before deciding. "Sam." He waited for her to look at him. "Dacia went out fifteen minutes ago. She's not back." He dragged his hand through his hair and felt it fall into place. "Gonna look for her."

"Do you want me to come?" She yawned.

He shook his head. "Nah. No sense in no one getting sleep."

He opened the door and peeked out, making sure nobody was in the hallway. Then he hurried for the stairwell. He scanned each floor for her, wondering where she would have gone.

When he got to the main floor, he stared out the glass doors. She shouldn't have gone outside. She should have known better, but lately, she seemed to have a penchant for recklessness.

He stood there with his hands on his hips, debating whether he should leave the building or not when his mind was made up for him.

Voices came from the staircase. With each second, they grew louder, closer. He pushed through the door, tucked his hands into his pockets, and walked along the sidewalk like he was just out for a stroll.

It was a clear, crisp night. Stars crowded the sky. Some of the tension in his shoulders released, and he breathed easier. Maybe Dacia had just lost track of time. Maybe not coming back had nothing to do with Nefarious. Maybe she was still in the building in one of the many restrooms or just on the opposite side of the halls he'd walked down.

Maybe.

But he couldn't take that chance.

Instead of sleeping, he spent the night scouring every inch of campus for Dacia. At 7:30, he found himself in front of Cacomistle Hall. He looked up at the stone and timber building debating on whether or not he should let Sarah know that Dacia was gone.

Finally, having decided it was the right thing to do, he trudged up the open staircase. Telling Sarah that he had failed both her and Dacia was the last thing he wanted to do, but he needed to own up to it.

He stood in the hallway outside of Sarah's office, listening to voices behind the door. Closing his eyes, he prayed that one of them belonged to Dacia, that she had come here again.

He rapped his knuckles against the wood, then rocked back on his heels. *Please, please, please.*

Sarah opened the door, and his heart plummeted. Nurse Heron sat on the couch where Dacia usually positioned herself. She held a cup of coffee in her hands and looked at Cody over her shoulder.

"Just one second, Nancy." Sarah stepped into the hallway, pulling the door shut behind her. "What is it, Cody?" She rested her hand on his upper arm.

He looked down at his feet. "She's gone."

"How long?" Sarah's grip tightened as her fingers curled, digging through his sweatshirt.

He kept staring at his shoes. Maybe he should have called her right away, but if Sarah had gone out in the middle of the night and something had happened to her again, Dacia wouldn't have been there to save her. "Around 1:00."

"Okay." Her eyes flashed, and he could see that she wanted to say more, but she just looked over her shoulder. "I'll tell Nancy I need to go so I can help you look for her."

He shook his head. "I've searched everywhere." He crossed one arm over his body and gripped the opposite elbow. "Think I'll go back to her room for a bit. See if she shows up."

"Let me know if you need anything." She pinched her lips together and stood with her hands on her hips. "What was she thinking?"

Cody's shoulders slumped. "Said she needed to walk around. Was gonna stay in the building and be back in fifteen minutes." He pressed his eyes closed and dropped his chin to his chest. "She promised."

"She'll turn up, Cody." Sarah took his hand in hers. "I'll have the staff keep an eye out for her. You should try to get some rest."

Cody trudged back to the dorm. He hadn't really thought he would find her, but he had hoped, and now, without that hope, all he had were worry and fear. He made it to the outside door before realizing that it was early in the morning, and he had no key. Samantha would probably kick his butt if he woke her up … unless she was already awake, wondering if he had found Dacia.

He pulled the door open and went inside. If she wasn't up already, he would apologize.

Chapter 17

By mid-afternoon, Cody was frantic. Dacia hadn't shown up. Samantha had searched all the restrooms in the building. She'd knocked on doors, asking if anyone had seen her. They had looked everywhere they could think of, and there was no sign of her anywhere.

Samantha had let Cody into her room while she checked the restrooms again. He had only been back for a few minutes when he heard someone whimper. He turned around and saw Dacia crouched on the floor with her head bowed.

"Dacia"—Cody's voice came out gruffer than he'd intended—"where've you been? How'd you get here?"

She glanced up at him. Then her gaze darted around the room. Her eyes were wide open and wild. She reminded him of a rabbit just before it darts off, zigging and zagging, trying to outmaneuver its hunter.

He moved slowly, afraid that he might scare her off. Holding his hands up in front of himself, he sat next to her. He inched closer, and when she didn't back away, he wrapped his arms around her. His breath hitched when his fingers touched her back. Her shirt was ripped open, and what he assumed was blood coated his fingers. "You're here. You're okay," he whispered directly into her ear. Her heart pounded against his chest, feeling more like a bird trying to flee its cage than a pulse.

She stared straight ahead, not even acknowledging his presence. Then she closed her eyes, and her body shuddered.

Cody pulled her closer, whispering in her ear and rubbing her arm, hoping to soothe some of her pain, all the while wondering what had happened to her.

Her trembling eventually slowed.

"Please say something … anything." He slid one arm under her legs and lifted. "Oh, my God, Dacia—" he nearly dropped her "—what happened?"

She stared down at her mutilated leg without saying anything. Then her body went limp in Cody's arms.

Careful not to jostle her leg too much, he lifted her. Cradling her against his body, he carried her to Cookie Monster. He brought over the footstool that Samantha kept her socks in and propped Dacia's leg up on it. Then he knelt on the floor beside her, holding her hand, gently rubbing his thumb over hers, taking in her dirt and blood-splattered clothes, and wondering what had happened to her.

The door opened, and Samantha said, "She's not—" Her gaze darted from the blood on the carpet, to Cody, and then to Dacia. "Did you call Sarah?"

"N—" Cody had to swallow over the lump in his throat before he could even get one word out. "Not yet." He closed his eyes and tried to calm his racing heart. "She's messed up."

Samantha nodded and walked straight to the phone. Cody tuned her out, focusing all of his attention on Dacia. *Wake up,* he thought over and over again.

Big Bird rocked back when Samantha sat. "Where was she?"

"Hasn't said anything." Cody shook his head. "Got no answers, only questions."

He felt Samantha's gaze on them as he quietly willed Dacia to wake up, but he didn't look at her, didn't take his focus off of Dacia. Even in sleep, her breathing was erratic. He rubbed his free hand over her uninjured leg, hoping his touch might soothe her even a little.

Finally, her eyes fluttered open. She looked around like she was confused about where she was.

Thank you. He glanced up at the ceiling. Then still gently caressing her hand, he said, "Sarah's on her way over." His voice sounded foreign to him, strained and husky.

Dacia nodded, then reached for her leg. Instead, her hands clenched the arms of the chair, digging into it. Sweat beaded on her temples. She seemed to gather herself, and ever so slowly, she slid her hands along the towel that he had used to cover her leg. She didn't move it, just closed her eyes and concentrated.

Cody watched her, wondering if she would say anything.

There was a knock at the door, and Dacia jerked upright, grasping Cody's hand, clenching his fingers in a vise-like grip.

He lifted his lips into a ghost of a smile and brushed a lock of her hair back, tucking it behind her ear. "Dacia, it's okay."

Samantha got up and let Sarah in. "Watch your step."

Sarah glanced at the floor and, without a word, stepped over Dacia's blood. She sat in Big Bird, leaning as close to Dacia as she could. She rested her elbows on her knees and folded her hands together. Looking Dacia over from head to toe.

Cody lifted the towel, and Sarah didn't react at all.

"Back of her shirt is shredded." Cody carefully laid the towel over Dacia's leg before threading his fingers through hers again. "Hasn't said a word."

"I know …" Dacia's words were hard to make out. Her voice was hoarse and barely audible. "You want me to tell you what happened, but I'm still trying to figure it out myself."

"Dacia"—Sarah reached over and took hold of Dacia's other hand—"I think you are in shock. Would you like to go see Nancy or go to the hospital?"

"Uh … no. Bad idea." The look Dacia gave her made it clear that she thought that was the dumbest thing she had ever heard.

"Think about it." Sarah pulled her hand back.

"No." She dragged her fingers through her hair and winced when she touched the back of her head. "If it heals right away, how am I supposed to explain it? The doctors will think they're going crazy if they see two miraculous recoveries in such a short time."

"I'm just trying to help you." Sarah raised her hands in surrender. "Why don't we get you cleaned up?"

A door slammed in the hallway, and Dacia jumped, jerking her head around. Once again, her eyes were wide.

"Dacia"—remembering the injured fox he had found several years ago, Cody tried to make his voice as soothing as he could—"it was just a door. You're okay." He fought to keep his expression neutral. He didn't want her to see how worried he was. He needed to be strong for her.

She looked down at her lap. "I keep waiting to wake up. This has to be a nightmare."

Samantha walked to the refrigerator and pulled a bottle of water out. She handed it to Dacia, smiling meekly at her.

As Dacia lifted the bottle to her lips, she winced. "I walked around, but I needed fresh air. I just stood outside the door and looked up at the stars." She didn't meet anyone's eyes. "I was talking to myself, and Bryce answered. Then he hit me on the back of the head."

Cody ground his teeth. There were so many things he would like to say, but he didn't want to interrupt Dacia for fear that she would stop talking.

"When I woke up, my head pounded, I was tied to a chair, and there was a bright light shining right in my eyes." She sounded like the living dead. There was no inflection in her voice at all. "I tried to use my powers, but nothing happened. Every time I tried, the throbbing got worse."

Her hand trembled as she lifted her water bottle to her mouth. "I tried to picture the lake, to calm myself, but when I thought about it, it was stormy. The water crashed against the rocks."

Cody took her hand in his and gently rubbed circles over the back of it.

"There was the sound of distant thunder, and the amulet started glowing." Dacia started breathing harder and faster. "I shattered the chair and freed myself. When I turned away from the light, I realized I was in a cave. There were stalagmites and stalactites all around me, and there was only one way out of the cavern. I ran through it and up a path. Then I hid in a crack."

Cody wanted to hold her, to reassure her that she was fine. She had made it out, but he was afraid to touch her back or her leg or her head. He was afraid she had more injuries that she hadn't told them about yet.

"He could smell me." She stopped and half-heartedly lifted her shoulder. "Well, he said he could smell my fear. He tried to compel me to move out into the open, but I stayed hidden until I heard his whip crack." If at all possible, her voice became even more monotonous. "I jumped out, hoping not to get hit by it, but I was an idiot. He wasn't by me."

She stared straight ahead, never blinking, and Cody wondered if this could be a symptom of shock. Could it take all of her emotions from her and turn her into a robot?

"I ran away from him, and he cracked the whip again." She jerked her leg back and clenched her jaw. Her fingers dug into the arm of the chair.

"Take your time, Dacia." Cody knelt next to her and breathed the words into her ear. "It's okay."

Sarah reached forward. "You're here with us. You'll be all right."

She finally had some inflection in her voice when she looked at Sarah and said, "No, I won't. I can't beat Nefarious. I won't get out alive again."

Nobody argued with her.

"The whip wrapped around my ankle." She shuddered. "His skin glowed like the dying embers in a campfire, flickering from black to red. He dragged me toward him, and the rock floor gouged my back." She clutched Cody's hand. "I shot ice at the whip, but Nefarious flicked his wrist, moving it to the side. I was too close to him." Her words started rushing out, and her pulse pounded in her neck. "I filled the pathway between us with ice, making a wall, then slammed my foot down on the ground and shattered the whip. I flew through the cave, but I didn't get very far before he destroyed the barrier." Her words ran over each other in their rush to escape her mouth.

"Breathe," Cody reminded her.

She sucked in two deep breaths. "He roared, and rocks fell from the ceiling and walls. I made it out of the cave right before boulders crashed down. Unfortunately, so did he." She pressed her eyes closed, quickly opening them again. The whites showed all around her irises.

He rubbed his chest, hoping to alleviate the sharp pain that was lodged behind his rib cage. Every word she said, every detail she described made his throat tighten painfully. He needed to take this from her, but how? How could he trade places with her?

"He lunged." She wrapped her arm around her stomach. "His claws tore through the charred skin on my leg. I thought I was going to pass out from the pain." She reached her other hand toward her leg but stopped when it stretched her back. "I used my powers to pick up rocks from the ground and throw them at him. It was enough to get him to let go."

Neither Sarah nor Samantha said anything. They just watched Dacia. Samantha's already pale skin had lost all of its color. Sarah's hazel eyes and mouth sagged with what Cody assumed was sympathy.

"He roared, and flames erupted all over his body, blasting me with a wave of heat." She took another drink. "I didn't know what to do, so I kept throwing rocks at him. Somehow, he started an inferno behind me. I couldn't back up, and I couldn't go forward."

Samantha fiddled with her necklace, pulling the pendant on it back and forth over the chain. "Dacia, you're white as a ghost. Are you going to be okay? Can I get you something?"

She shook her head and closed her eyes, snapping them open once again. She wiped her sleeve over her face. "He pulled his sword, and he, uh—" she sucked in a deep breath "—he swung it at me. It was like a scene straight out of a movie. The sword moved in slow motion, and the rest of the world moved at its usual pace. I looked down at campus and thought how much I would like to be here. I was about to die, but then I was kneeling on the carpet, and Cody was frantic, and it was too good to be true." She held her hand up with her thumb and forefinger barely spread apart. "I was this close to death."

Cody needed to be closer to her. He pulled himself to his feet and looked her over, trying to determine the best way to hold her without causing her harm. He sat on the arm of the chair and pulled her to him, tracing circles over her arm. His eyes filled with tears.

She looked up at him, begging him for the answer she so desperately needed to hear. "So, when am I going to wake up?"

No one answered. What could they possibly say?

"All my past dreams seemed so realistic, so today, I kept expecting to wake up. When the whip wrapped around my leg and I didn't, part of me knew it wasn't a dream, but the other part of me prayed it was." She stared out the window, but by the blank look on her face, Cody didn't think she saw anything. At least nothing here. "I don't—" She closed her eyes and leaned her head back.

"Dacia, take all the time you need." Samantha shot her a reassuring smile, but Cody doubted Dacia saw it. "We understand how difficult this is for you. With all you've gone through, you have plenty of reasons to cry or scream or throw a temper tantrum or whatever you need to do. Somehow you have to relieve some of your frustration."

"I can't go around crying all the time." Dacia swiped at her eyes. "What am I supposed to do, drown Nefarious in a river of tears? If you were watching a movie and the hero had a meltdown every other scene, wouldn't you think, 'What a wuss!'?"

"This isn't a movie." Cody placed his hand over the top of hers. He didn't know how to comfort someone who had been attacked by a demon, but he figured his touch might help mollify her. "This is your life. No one is paying you to play a part. You were thrown into it and have every right to get upset."

"He's right." Samantha nodded her agreement. "I don't know how you deal with this at all. You're so much stronger than you think. Give yourself a little credit."

Dacia looked at Sarah as if expecting her to say something. When she didn't, Dacia said, "What I wanted to say earlier was Nefarious is *huge* and *strong* and *fast* and … pure *evil*. I guess that's the best way to describe him. The hero in the diary tried to use lightning against him. I tried ice." She pushed up her sleeve, then pulled it back down. "I'm, uh, pretty sure fire won't work against him. After a few rocks hit him in the head, they didn't seem to bother him. I'm out of ideas, and I think … well, I … I think I'm about out of time, too." The last several words were spoken in a hurry as if she was afraid she wouldn't be able to get them out otherwise.

Sarah patted Dacia's uninjured leg. "I don't know how you will defeat Nefarious, but you have proven you can hold your own."

"How do—"

Sarah held her hand up and spoke with a stern tone. "Please, let me finish. You made it out alive, injured but alive. You found a new power, and if need be, you can teleport out of danger again. I know you're frustrated and discouraged, but it will get better. Now, I would like to see your leg." She stood and eased the towel from it.

Liquid seeped out of the wound. Two cuts reached from her ankle to her knee. Cody could see her muscles and bones. He wanted to look away, but he couldn't force himself to.

"It's not healing." Dacia pulled her hand through her mussed hair. "I healed the two of you faster than I'm healing myself."

Sarah sat again. She gazed at Dacia's leg for an eternity or a few seconds. The way time was moving, it was hard to tell. "Your injury is severe."

"Oh, I'm sorry if I'm being unrealistic." Dacia folded her arms over her chest and glared at Sarah. "After all, you were dead. Something tells me no matter how mangled my leg is, dead is worse."

Sarah shook her head and gave Dacia one of those looks that all mothers had mastered. The kind that let you know exactly how ridiculous you were acting. "Maybe it's a little harder to repair flesh and muscles that have been burned and sliced apart than it is to make somebody breathe or start the heart pumping again. Hmm—" she rubbed her chin "—it seems to me even doctors, at times, have more trouble with that. I've never seen stitches come out the same day they went in, but I have seen people receive mouth-to-mouth resuscitation and be fine after just a short time."

"Cody's cuts healed quickly," Dacia rebutted. "I'm sure Dr. Sequoia will attest to that."

Sarah glanced at Cody and tilted her head. He knew she was going to say that his wounds had nothing on Dacia's, and even though he knew she was right, he felt his hackles rise. "Cody's injuries were serious. However, his cuts did not tear through muscle and weren't clear to the bone. Yours were also caused by a demon. That, in my opinion, could be a very significant factor."

Cody relaxed ever so slightly. He agreed completely with what she'd said.

"How's your head?" Samantha asked.

Dacia haltingly lifted her hand to the back of her head, looking like she was afraid to know the answer. "It seems to be fine."

"Maybe Sarah's right about the demon thing then." Samantha shrugged. "I suppose it's possible his magic counteracts yours somehow."

"Maybe not magic." Cody rubbed his chin. "Maybe venom or something."

"I just hope it heals soon." Dacia looked down at her hands. "I hope I'm making the right decision about the doctor." A tear slipped from her eye.

Cody brushed it off her cheek, allowing his hand to linger against her skin. "We all hope so."

"Let's get this bandaged." Sarah stood and rubbed her hands together

"We can take care of it." Samantha set her hand on Sarah's. "You should get back before it gets dark. Dacia won't be able to save you tonight."

"Are you sure?" Sarah looked from Samantha to Cody.

"Yeah. Oh, and I'll be sleeping there." Cody pointed at Big Bird. He was ready to fight with Sarah over this if he needed to, and if she escorted him out, he would just come back as soon as she was out of sight. "Hope you don't mind."

"For the record, Cody, you cannot be in the girls' dorm after midnight." She shook her finger at him. "Unofficially, I think it's a great idea. We all need to watch out for each other."

Cody let out a deep breath and relaxed. "Want me to walk you back?"

"Thank you. No." Sarah patted Dacia's hand, then walked away. "I'll be fine." She stopped before reaching the door. "I forgot about this." She pointed at the floor. "Do you want help cleaning the blood?"

"No." Samantha stood with her hands on her hips and shook her head at Sarah like she was a toddler who just couldn't take no for an answer. "You need to get going. Me and Cody will take care of it. Right, Cody?"

"No, I'll do it." Dacia fought to hold a yawn in, but it escaped. "It's my blood, not yours."

"Dacia, you'll sit there 'til your leg heals." Cody pointed at the chair. "We'll take care of you. You have to let us."

Sarah nodded at Dacia, saying, "Let them help you." Her expression softened into that of a concerned mother before she added, "And, get some rest."

Chapter 18

Cody wasn't cut out to be a doctor or nurse. He tried to gently clean and wrap Dacia's leg, but every time she flinched, he just hurt her more. Samantha ended up taking over, and Cody knelt on the floor. Dacia clenched her teeth and crushed his hand every time Samantha dabbed at her wound.

Her eyes grew heavier with each passing second, and as soon as her leg was bandaged, she fell into a fitful sleep.

Cody watched her for a while. Her head jerked from side to side, and her eyes moved rapidly beneath her closed lids. He was afraid she would hurt herself, but there was nothing he could do for her.

He stepped away, looking over his shoulder as he walked toward the blood staining the floor. Samantha was working on cleaning it up. He got down on his hands and knees and started scrubbing.

By the time they finished, both of them were covered in blood. Samantha washed her hands in the sink before grabbing her bathroom bag. "I'm going to get a shower. Need anything?"

"Nah." He rubbed soap all over his hands and arms. "I'll keep an eye on her." He nodded toward Dacia.

Samantha gave him an understanding nod, the kind you give when you have no idea what to say. "Hopefully, she'll just keep sleeping."

As soon as she left the room, Cody pulled his shirt off and soaked it in cold water. Dacia's blood pulled away from the fibers, mixing with the water, and running down the drain. He wrung it out and set it in the sink. Then he grabbed his sweatpants out of his duffel and changed into them. He sat in Big Bird and stretched his legs out in front of him, leaning his head against the back of the chair.

He'd only had his eyes closed for a few minutes when Dacia screamed. He leapt up and rushed to her side. "Dacia, breathe." He pried her fingers loose from the arm of the chair and squeezed her hand. Brushing the hair off of her face, he spoke as quietly as he could, trying to keep her from panicking. "You're going to hyperventilate."

Through panting breaths, she said, "Just a nightmare."

"Not your nightmares." He fought to remain calm, keeping his fingers light on her skin. "Your nightmares are dangerous … life-threatening nightmares."

Grimacing, she pressed her eyes closed. "What's your point?"

"Don't pass it off as just a nightmare." He cupped her cheek, then gently caressed her face, hoping his touch would calm her. "They're a big deal."

"She was there," Dacia murmured.

Cody's hand stilled for just a moment. "Who?"

She stared at him for several seconds before shaking her head. "Cassandra. I can't believe she just watched him try to kill me."

"What?" His hand slipped, and he fell back on his heels.

"She hid behind the bushes. I didn't notice when it happened, but in my dream, I saw her as plain as day." She tugged her hands through her hair, then clasped them in her lap. "Everything Nefarious or I said or did was exactly the way I remember it, down to the last detail. I probably saw her, but it didn't connect." She pressed her eyes closed. "I'm sure she was there, though."

Cody rubbed the back of his neck. He didn't know how somebody could stand by and watch someone get hurt like that, but then again, she had not only watched but helped the others beat him. "Not good."

"Where's Samantha?" Dacia looked up into Samantha's loft, but the bed was still made from that morning.

He took her hand in his again. "Washing. We got covered in blood."

She threw the blanket to the side and gasped.

"What's wrong?" Cody asked.

She nodded at her leg. The bandages were soaked. They should have expected that. Whenever she got injured in a dream these days, she got injured in reality. He should have looked her over as soon as she screamed.

Rocking back on his heels, Cody said, "I'll get something to stop the bleeding."

"Just use the blanket." She leaned her head back and closed her eyes. "It's probably covered already."

He grabbed it and looked at his bloody hand. "Yeah. Bandages off or blanket on top of them?"

"Just cover it. I'll take the bandages off when it stops bleeding." She clenched her teeth.

Cody set the blanket over her leg and tried not to hurt her too badly.

She inhaled sharply.

"Sorry." He winced, pinching his eyebrows together.

"I know, but it hurts like hell," she said.

After a few minutes, Cody released the pressure.

Dacia fainted.

Cody grabbed one of Dacia's pillows and a blanket off of her bed and lay on the floor next to her.

Samantha watched him with her head tipped toward one shoulder. "Why not sleep in her loft?"

"Want to be close in case she needs me." He looked at Dacia, and his heart clenched. She was sleeping but no better than she had earlier.

Samantha reached over and turned her lamp off. "Suit yourself."

Cody closed his eyes. It didn't take long for him to fall asleep and start dreaming about Dacia fighting an enormous, winged beast. The nightmare played out just like she had described. This time, though, he was there to witness it all. He lay on the rocky ground incapable of helping her. His smashed knee kept him from standing. His ribs ached with each breath he took. He watched through swollen eyes, not wanting to see, but not capable of looking away.

The monster was relentless. Dacia fought back courageously at first, but the demon wore her down, draining her energy, and sapping her strength.

Dacia's shrill scream tore through Cody's dream.

He jumped up, instantly awake. "Dacia." He stood above her in the darkened room. "You okay?"

"What time is it?" Her voice was rough.

"It's, uh, 2:33 Monday morning." He knelt beside her. His heart pounded against his chest, trying to flee his rib cage. He tried to be calm, but he needed her answer. "Are. You. Okay?"

"Nefarious threatened to get to me through my friends."

Samantha jerked upright in bed and switched on her lamp. "Us?"

Dacia nodded. "He said because I got away, he wouldn't go easy on me or my friends." She stared at her trembling hands. "I'm sorry."

Samantha's initial shock wore off. "Not all your dreams come true."

"Yeah … maybe." Dacia shot Samantha a shaky smile, but Cody saw right through it.

Cody cupped her chin in his hand, turning her face toward him. She still hadn't answered, and he needed to know. "Are you hurt?"

She shook her head. "Nothing new."

His muscles relaxed, making him unintentionally rock back on his heels. He breathed easy for the first time since she woke him up.

"Do you need anything?" Samantha asked.

Even in the dim lighting of the room, Cody could see that her face had turned red. His head dipped toward his shoulder, and his eyebrows pulled together. He had no idea why that question would embarrass her. "What?"

She turned away. "Glacier," she answered in a small voice.

Cody climbed her loft ladder, grabbed her white teddy bear, and handed it to her. "You're so cute when you're embarrassed."

"Yeah, sure." She took the stuffed animal from him and snuggled with it.

Dacia cringed with every step she took. Even if he hadn't been bearing most of her weight, he would have known how much pain she was in. Her sharp intakes of breath and her pinched expression gave her away. He'd offered to carry her, but she insisted on walking, or more accurately, limping.

She'd tried to get him to stay behind. He wasn't supposed to be in the dorms, and if he got caught, things would become a whole lot more difficult on everyone, but he wasn't about to let her go on her own.

He fought the urge to hurry through the empty hallway, knowing that speed would hurt her even more. He would face the consequences, whatever they were, if they got caught. It was worth it to be able to help her, to be there for her.

Cody sat in the stairwell, hiding in the shadows, hoping to remain unnoticed until he had to walk Dacia back to her room. There was a noise in the hallway. He carefully peeked around until he saw Dacia waiting for him. He jumped up and hurried to her side. Her hair was hidden beneath a purple towel. Her skin glistened where she hadn't dried it completely.

She took a couple of steps toward him.

"Hey … you're not limping." He looked down at her feet and then into her eyes. Something about her gait was off, but she didn't seem to be in pain anymore. "Your leg better?"

"No." She levitated until she was taller than him.

"Oh. Why didn't you do that before?" He rubbed his neck hard enough to loosen some of the knots in it. "Not that I minded holding you."

"I hate to break it to you." She dropped back down until she was barely off the ground. "You're dating an idiot." Resting her head on his shoulder, they went back to her room, making much better time than they had going there. "But I didn't mind leaning on you either."

Cody stepped inside just as a door opened down the hallway. He looked out through the peephole. "That was close," he whispered. "Marcy's patrolling."

"Don't be surprised if she stops by and asks if you're here."

He watched Dacia pull the towel off her head. Her wet hair was dark, nearly black with a red tint. He'd heard what she'd said, but until someone knocked on the door, it hadn't registered.

Cody scrambled up into Dacia's loft, pressing against the wall and surrounding himself with blankets and pillows.

The door opened a crack. "Oh, hi, Marcy. What's up?" Dacia whispered.

"Cody's not in here, is he?"

He imagined her pigtails bobbing as she tried to peek around Dacia.

"No." Her voice didn't shake. The word didn't rise at the end like she was asking a question.

When did she get that good at lying? Cody wondered. Then he realized, she probably always had been. She'd had to hide her powers from everyone but him until just recently.

"I could've sworn I heard him in the hall." Marcy sounded like she was doubting herself.

"I just got back from showering, and Samantha's still in bed. I'd appreciate it if you didn't wake her. She gets grumpy when she doesn't get enough sleep."

After the door clicked shut, Cody waited a few seconds to climb down from Dacia's loft. "How did you know?"

She chuckled, covering her mouth and glancing at Saman-tha. "Marcy doesn't patrol the halls, and the only rule she has ever seemed to care about is the hours guys can't be in here."

"Maybe because she's never been on a date." Cody rolled his eyes and stepped closer to Dacia.

"Now, be nice." She gave him a stern look that crumpled into a grin as she smacked his arm. "She's just doing her job. Besides, I'm not sure I've been on a date yet—" she rubbed her chin thoughtfully "—or do you call sitting in my room eating pizza a date?"

Heat crept onto his cheeks. "What about putt-putt?"

"If that counts"—she turned a scalding look on him—"I have to call this relationship off."

"Wha—"

She crossed her arms over her chest and tapped her foot, soundlessly since it was an inch above the ground. "If that was a date, you're two-timing me."

His mouth fell open, and he floundered for words. What was that supposed to mean? He stared at her, wondering if she'd taken some damage from the blow to her head. She had to know he'd never cheat on her. Didn't she?

"You did pay for Samantha to come along, didn't you?"

"Yeah." He covered his mouth with his palm and rubbed his face. "But, it should count." Everything suddenly clicked into place, and he realized she was giving him crap.

"No, a date would just be the two of us." Walking her fingers up his chest, she said, "Me and you … alone."

His skin tingled beneath her touch. "Okay." He pressed his hand against hers, flattening it over his heart. "Next Saturday dinner and a movie, just us."

She inched back and fanned her face with her hand. "Why, Cody Hawks, are you asking me out? That would be delightful."

It had been a long time since he had seen this playful version of Dacia and not at all since they'd been dating. He reached out and snatched a lock of her hair, holding it between his finger and his thumb. "Like the wet hair look." His eyes darkened. He dropped her curl, settled his hands on her waist, and eliminated the thin strip of air that had separated them. His body pressed against hers. He brought his mouth down.

And Dacia gasped. She jerked away, and he realized his mistake.

Still holding onto her, he backed away. "I wasn't thinking. I'm s—"

She covered his mouth and swallowed. "I know. Help me out of these"—she tugged at her pajama bottoms—"so I can sit."

Was she really asking him to undress her? He stared at her, and his heart raced.

"I have shorts on." She pushed his chin up so that he was looking her in the eyes.

"Yeah … right." His hands were suddenly all thumbs. He closed his eyes, sucked in a deep breath, then pulled her pajama pants down to her knees, easing the fabric over her wound, trying not to touch it.

She closed her eyes and clutched his shoulders.

He slipped the PJs over her feet and stared at her injured leg. Her pain had to be excruciating. The wound was jagged, brutal, but without all the blood and gore surrounding it, it didn't look quite as bad as it had yesterday.

He helped her sit in Cookie Monster and propped her leg up on the stool.

"Just because I got more blood cleaned off it." The liveliness was gone from her voice now.

He didn't blame her. "Sure you don't wanna go to the hospital to get something for your pain?" If he could take it from her, he would, but unfortunately, that was her gift, not his.

"And risk falling asleep there?" She snorted. "If it knocked me out, would I wake up from my nightmares before he killed me?"

He hadn't thought of that. What would they think if she got injured while sleeping? What would they do to her?

He sat in Big Bird, slowly rocking back and forth.

Voices from the hallway drifted through the thin walls. He pulled his phone out to check the time. 5:54.

Looking from Dacia to the door, he dragged his hand down his face. He didn't want to leave her alone, but he had a test in Geography.

He rubbed the back of his neck. "I gotta go." It was going to be hard getting past everyone without getting caught. "Need to go to class."

"I'm not." She combed her fingers through her hair and pulled it into a ponytail. "I'm going through the journals. There's got to be something helpful in them."

He watched her for a long moment, wondering what kind of trouble she could get herself into while he was gone. "Promise you won't leave?" He felt like a broken record, but he needed to ask. Maybe one of these times, she would stay true to her word.

She crossed her heart. "I won't. I don't plan on doing anything stupid until my leg heals. Then, hopefully, after that, I still won't do anything stupid."

There was nothing more he could do, so he strode toward her, hoping he looked confident. He leaned down, cradled her face in his hands, and kissed her gently.

She clutched his shirt, pulling him closer. Then her hand fisted in the hair at the back of his head, and the languorous kiss became searing. Her tongue slipped between his lips, touching his.

Heat flared through his body as he deepened the kiss. He wanted to pull her closer still, but somehow, through the passion and desire, he remembered her crying out when his leg had touched hers, and he pulled away.

Her eyes shone as if lit by an inner fire.

He wanted nothing more than to crush his lips against hers, to hold her and never let go, but he would rather watch the whole world burn than to hurt her again, so before he could change his mind, he hurried through the door.

He practically sprinted through the halls. Darting outside, he stood in the cool morning air. He needed to get control of himself before he hurt her worse. He couldn't get that close to her again until her leg healed. He didn't want to cause her pain.

Hoping Drew would still be sleeping, he quietly pushed the door open. Drew was standing in his boxers, digging through the clothes on the floor, picking them up, and sniffing them. "Look at you." Drew dropped the t-shirt and picked up another. "Barely making it back in time to leave. Where've you been?" He wagged his eyebrows at Cody. "Is there some fire in that redhead of yours?"

More than you'll ever know, Cody thought. He was glad he'd taken other clothes with him to Dacia's room. He couldn't imagine what Drew would say if he'd returned covered in blood. "Nah, stayed up too late playing video games."

"Yeah." Drew pulled a black shirt over his head, then started looking for jeans. "Sure."

Cody grabbed clean clothes out of his dresser and wondered how anybody could live like Drew. It wasn't that difficult to do a load of laundry on occasion, but maybe his parents hadn't ever shown him how, or maybe he didn't mind stinking.

Cody hurried through his shower, went back to his room, grabbed his backpack, and less than an hour after leaving, he stood in the hallway outside of Dacia's room, knocking softly, hoping somebody would let him in before he was caught. "Let me in. Please."

He looked down the hall, shifting from foot to foot, trying to come up with an excuse for being there before he was supposed to be.

Samantha opened the door, looking over his shoulder at Dacia. "How's your leg?"

"Not good," she answered, and Cody's heart plummeted.

He hurried inside and pushed the door closed. "Thanks. Lot more girls in the hall at this time."

"Skipping class?" Samantha asked Dacia as she scrambled back into her loft.

She nodded. "Yeah."

Cody stood back, watching Dacia. He schooled his features into what he hoped was a blank expression.

"What?" she asked.

He nodded toward the door. "Told Samantha your leg isn't good. Because of me?"

"Because I was attacked by a demon from the Abyss." She shook her head while rolling her eyes. "Can you help me with it?"

He remembered how easily she had lied to Marcy after her shower, and he hoped she knew that no matter what, she could tell him the truth. He might not always like it or even take it well, but he wanted her to know she could trust him.

He grabbed the bandages and scooted the desk chair over. Ever so gently, he wrapped the gauze around her leg. Each time she jerked or winced, it felt like a punch in his gut, but he schooled his expression and hoped she wouldn't notice.

When he finished, he leaned back, folding his hands behind his head. "Need anything before I leave?"

"The amulet." She pointed at her bag.

He dug it out and draped it over his fingers, carrying it back to her. He hadn't really looked at it before. It was gaudy, ugly, and probably worth a small fortune.

Holding the necklace out of reach, he looked down at her, hoping that she could tell by his expression that he was begging. "Stay here."

Samantha climbed out of her loft. "I'm giving up on sleep for now. I'll be back." She grabbed her bathroom bag. "Don't leave."

"I don't have much choice." Dacia flipped her hands up in the air. "I couldn't even get the door."

Cody had three back-to-back classes, and his first two were in the same room with the same teacher, Dr. Andrew Cedar.

Cody tapped his foot against the tiles, impatiently waiting for his test. He shouldn't have come. He should have stayed with Dacia. What if she fell asleep and had another nightmare? What if she decided to leave?

The exam popped up on his laptop, and he answered the questions that he could. He knew the answers. They were stored somewhere in his head, but his mind kept wandering back to Dacia. He should have stayed with her. He needed to make sure she was okay. Either way, he was failing this test, so he should have done what was right.

He sat through two excruciating hours of class, imagining all of the horrors Dacia could be going through while he pretended to care whether or not he passed either Geography or American History.

As soon as class was dismissed, he jogged from Primrose Hall back to Wisteria Hall. It was late enough now that he was allowed to be there. He stood in front of Dacia's door with his hand raised in the air, ready to knock, when Samantha opened it. "Hi. Leaving?"

"No, opening the door for you." She grinned at him.

He looked over her head at Dacia sitting in Cookie Monster and realized she must have alerted Samantha to his presence. He strode toward Dacia, staying far enough away that he wouldn't be tempted to touch her. "Any better?"

"About the same." She shrugged. "I don't know how it looks."

He stared at her mummy-wrapped leg. How long would it take to heal? Was her magic gone? Was it too depleted to heal the wound? Or was there something more to it? Was demon venom a thing? "Thought it'd be better."

"Yeah …" She looked at it, then away quickly. "I need to talk to Sarah."

Samantha pointed at herself then Cody. "Why don't we get lunch while you call her?"

Cody took the phone out of its cradle and carried it over to her. He stood back from her while he gathered his self-restraint. Then he took two steps forward, handed the phone to her, quickly planted a kiss on the top of her head, and stepped away before she could stop him. *Be strong,* he thought to himself.

Chapter 19

"Dacia, wake up." Cody stood above her, shaking her shoulders. Her nightmares seemed to be worsening. Before her injury, she'd had a few a week, but not nightly. Now, she was having several in one day. "You're having a nightmare."

Her eyes shot open. Wild. Frantic. "Let go of me!"

He dropped her arms and stepped away. He didn't know if she was still in the dream or why she was yelling at him.

"I'm sorry, Cody." She pulled the blanket to the side, revealing her arm to him. The sleeve of her sweatshirt was gone, and she was burned from her shoulder to her wrist. Blackened, charred skin oozed a clear liquid.

"Sorry." He'd hurt her. He'd made her injuries worse. "You screamed. I wanted to wake you before anything happened." He stared at her. If she got this injured in her dreams, would she make it? Could she defeat the demon?

She raked her shaking fingers through her hair. "I didn't mean to yell at you."

He clenched his fists and released them, willing his hands to stop trembling. Then he grabbed the gauze and carefully wrapped Dacia's arm.

Samantha's alarm clock buzzed, and Dacia jumped. Samantha smacked it and rolled to a sitting position. "I thought—" she yawned and stretched "—I thought I'd get to go back to sleep. You okay, Dacia?"

"Been better." She pulled the blanket back up, hiding her wound. "I'm skipping again today."

Samantha looked over the side of her bed. "Your grades are going to plummet."

"Probably." Dacia held her hands up like two sides of a scale. "Good grades." She tipped her hands as if weighing her options. "Save the world."

Knowing that she had to feel a bit like Atlas right now, Cody patted her knee. "If anybody can do both, it's you."

She rolled her eyes. "Help me down the hall?"

"No problem." He helped Dacia move her injured leg to the floor. Then she lifted her good arm over his shoulders, putting all of her weight on him as he hoisted her out of the chair. Once she was up, she levitated herself so that her feet were just above the ground. While she hovered over the carpet, he went to her closet and pulled out a new hoodie.

She moaned as she pulled it on, but he knew she wouldn't want people to see her burnt sleeve and bandaged arm. They passed a few people in the hall, but nobody seemed to notice that Dacia wasn't touching the ground.

Marcy was just returning to her room as they neared it. She shot Cody a nasty look and said, "Make sure you're out of here on time tonight. I have a test in the morning and don't want to be up all night because you can't read a clock."

"According to my watch—" he glanced at his wrist, pretending to look at a watch that wasn't there "—it's a little early for you to start harassing me, so back off."

Marcy stepped inside her room and slammed the door before Cody could say anything else.

He looked down at Dacia and lifted his shoulder toward his ear. He wasn't in the mood to be harassed. His only goal had been to make it through the day without hurting Dacia, and he had completely blown it. "It's a little early, isn't it?"

"Yeah, but I'm the sarcastic one." She pointed at her chest. "You can't take that away from me. It's all I've got. Now everyone who doesn't already is going to start thinking I'm a bad influence on you."

His lip twitched up, but he bowed his head to hide it. "I'll do better."

When they got back, Cody helped Dacia get situated in Cookie Monster. Then he walked to the sink and brushed his teeth. He watched Dacia in the mirror. She stared at nothing. Her eyes held a faraway, vacant look. How much could she take before she broke? How many more injuries could she sustain before she decided to give into them? Everyone had a limit. How close was she to hitting hers?

He noticed when her eyes widened like she'd had an epiphany. His stomach dropped like an elevator falling to the ground floor. If it had something to do with defeating Nefarious, she would have shared it with them, but when she didn't, he realized she was hiding something from him again.

He rinsed his toothbrush off, then strode toward her, giving her a chance to tell him what she'd been thinking. When she didn't say anything by the time he got to her, he sighed and rested his hand on her shoulder. "You'll be okay?"

She tipped her head to the side. "Bored but fine."

"I know that look." He wiped his hand over his face. Didn't she realize it would kill him if something happened to her? Didn't she feel the same way about him? "Don't do it. Whatever it is. Please don't do it."

"You're not going to like it." She dragged her hand through her hair. "I thought about checking on Cassandra."

He clamped his mouth shut, grinding his teeth. He didn't want to say something he'd regret. Once the words were out of his mouth, he would be able to apologize for them, but he'd never be able to take them back. "Why?" He fought to keep his voice even. "What would possess you?"

She lowered her chin to her chest. "I … I need to figure out what's happening with her."

"You could get hurt." Cody's voice rose, and his posture stiffened. "Again." He took a deep breath and tried to calm himself. Yelling wouldn't do any good. Fighting wouldn't do any good. He needed to make her understand what she did to them when she snuck off. "We wouldn't have known where you went. Wouldn't know where to look for you! Why do you keep putting us through this? Why can't you just tell us what you're up to?"

Her eyes filled with tears. It broke his heart, but she need-ed to understand. "I'm sorry. I won't go."

"Dacia," Samantha said in a less agitated voice than Cody had used, "we don't want to see you get hurt again. We under-stand you need to figure out what's going on, but you have to trust us."

"That important, let's go after class." He couldn't believe he was saying it, but he'd do almost anything if it would stop her from crying.

She shook her head and wiped at her eyes. "The reason I was planning to go while you're in class is because they're all in there."

"Okay." He turned to Samantha. "Feel like playing hooky?"

"I, uh, I'd rather go to class."

"Oh, come on. Where's your spirit of adventure?" Dacia bit her bottom lip, obviously regretting the words.

Samantha narrowed her eyes, and her voice hardened. "My spirit of adventure disappeared a long time ago, and when you came back here the other day with your leg nearly ripped off, I lost even more of it. I expected you to lose some of yours, too."

Cody tilted his head to the side and nodded. He was glad Samantha had said it and not him. "Good point."

Samantha put her hand on Cody's arm. "Keep her safe, and watch out for yourself. I'll see you two at lunch."

Cody watched Samantha leave, feeling a little envious. He'd been planning on an uneventful day. He was going to go to class. Then he was going to spend the rest of the day with

Dacia, watching movies or playing games or whatever she wanted to do. He sat in Big Bird, leaning forward with his elbows resting on his knees. "What's your plan?"

"I, uh, kinda don't have one." Red tinted her cheeks, and even though he was frustrated with her, he had to admit that it was endearing. "I was winging this."

Cody stared at her, shaking his head. She never used to run headfirst into danger. She used to be cautious. "Any ideas at all?"

She shrugged, and the action was infuriating. "I suppose we should wait until class starts. Hopefully, Bryce, Vanessa, and Alvin go today. I'll knock on her door. If no one answers, I'll try to figure out how to get in. Otherwise, I'll make up a story about thinking it was someone else's room."

"That's your plan?" He leaned back and crossed his arms over his chest. She had planned on going by herself, but she hadn't given any thought to what she was actually going to do. Did she even know how she would get out of her chair on her own?

They sat in silence for the next fifteen minutes. Cody stared up at the ceiling or looked out the window. Pretty much anywhere but her. He was frustrated, but he would get over it.

Without a word, Cody stood. He reached his hand down, helping her stand. She balanced on her left leg until she lifted off the ground, keeping her injured leg from bearing any weight.

As they walked down the hallway, Cody thought, *What am I doing? Dacia's going to get herself killed, and I volunteered to go along for the ride—good thinking.*

"What did you say?" Dacia glared at him.

His brows pinched together, and he shook his head. "I didn't say anything."

"Oh." She paused. "I thought you said something to the effect of me getting myself killed and you volunteering to come along."

Cody stopped. He hadn't said that. He knew he hadn't. Rubbing his jaw, he asked, "How?" He looked down at her, then away. A storm brewed in her emerald eyes, and he didn't want to egg her on. "I didn't say that out loud."

"Well, you must've." She rose up to the same height as him. "Otherwise, I suppose I'd have a hard time hearing you, wouldn't I?"

He replayed the scene, wondering if he might have said it on accident, if it had slipped out, but he was sure he hadn't. That left only one explanation. "You read my mind … didn't you?"

She dropped back down to the ground and stared at her feet. "I don't know; I thought I heard you say it … I don't know what's up and what's down anymore. You were so quiet. I wondered what you were thinking, and you started talking. At first, I thought it was a coincidence." She reached toward him but dropped her hand before she touched him. "Please don't hate me. I couldn't bear that."

He closed the distance between them, holding her face in both of his hands, and wiped a tear from the corner of her eye with his thumb. "I love you too much to ever hate you." Did she seriously believe he could hate her? Just the thought of it sucked the breath from his lungs. He leaned his forehead against hers. "Sure you want to do this?"

Looking into his eyes, she placed her hands over the top of his. They were warm and soft, and he knew her answer before she said it. "I need to."

He tipped his head slightly, then started walking toward Cassandra's room. The sooner they got this over with, the sooner they could be done. He looked over his shoulder. She hadn't moved an inch.

"Dacia." Cody glanced back at her. She stood in the hallway, staring toward him like she had no idea he was even there. "Snap out of it."

"Sorry." She caught up to him. "I was just thinking."

He wrapped his arm around her shoulders. "No. You were spaced out." He would ask her what she was thinking, but he didn't know if he could handle her answer. For once, he wondered if he might be better off staying in the dark.

They stopped in front of Cassandra's door, and Cody waited for Dacia to decide what she was going to do. She lifted her hand, then dropped it, wiping her palm on her jeans. Then she raised her hand again and quickly knocked.

There was no sound on the other side of the door. Nobody answered. She knocked again.

The furnace kicked on. Heat hummed through the vent above their heads. Cody listened to it for several seconds. "Now what?"

"I'm working on it." Dacia glanced over her shoulder at him, closed her eyes, and placed her hands flat on the door.

He'd feel so much better if she had a plan. A way to get in and out without getting caught or hurt. He was about to suggest that they leave and come back later when Dacia stepped through the door. She hadn't opened it. She had just walked through it as if it didn't exist. "You okay?"

"Yeah … why wouldn't I be?" The wood between them muffled her voice.

He put his hands on the door, then rested his forehead against it. For eleven years, he had watched her start fires, change the weather, and make the earth shake, but now … there didn't seem to be any limit to what she could do. "You walked through the door … like it wasn't there."

He paced in the hallway, rubbing the back of his neck, wondering if he should try to go in, wondering why he hadn't told her to unlock it. He had just started back toward Cassandra's room when he heard a loud crash. He jogged the last few steps and knocked on the door. "Are you okay?"

"I will be." Her voice was strained, and he hated that he had no idea what was happening.

I will be.

He jiggled the doorknob. *I will be.* He held his hand up, wanting to pound on the door, but he stopped short. What if he distracted Dacia and something happened? He backed up and folded his arms over his chest. He couldn't get to her, couldn't help her at all. It was eerily silent until something hit the door. Shortly after, Dacia fell through it, landing flat on her back.

"Dacia." Cody hurried over to her. When she didn't answer, he picked her up and rushed her back to her room.

She looked up at him but said nothing. Then her head dropped back, and her eyes stared without seeing.

ଔ203ଓ

Chapter 20
Everything's Falling Apart

Cody carried Dacia back to her room and set her in Cookie Monster. Except for the rise and fall of her chest, she didn't move.

He sat across from her, staring at her, willing her to wake up. What had happened to her? Could she survive this? Was she strong enough? When despair clutched his heart, he decided to call Sarah.

He paced while waiting for Sarah to show up. What would have happened to Dacia if he hadn't gone with her? Would she still be lying in the hallway, or would Cassandra have gone after her?

A knock on the door interrupted his thoughts. As soon as he let Sarah in, she said. "Tell me what happened."

Cody told her the little he knew, never taking his eyes off of Dacia. When he finished, he stood next to her, taking her hand in his.

Samantha returned from class, looked around the room, and then dropped her chin to her chest as if defeated. "I knew this was a bad idea."

"She's awake," Sarah said with a sigh of relief. "Are you okay?"

Dacia nodded, then gripped the arms of the chair, closing her eyes.

Cody dropped to his knees. Tears blurred his vision, but he refused to let them fall. "Never do that again. Thought you were dying."

She cupped his cheek in her hand but said nothing. He looked her over wondering if he'd missed an injury, wondering for the Nth time what had gone on in Cassandra's room.

"What happened in there?" Samantha asked as if reading Cody's mind.

"I don't know," she answered in a dry, scratchy voice.

Cody turned toward Samantha. "Get her water. Please." He held onto Dacia's hand. Her fingers were ice cold.

She drank half of the water, looking over the bottle at Cody while she did. "The amulet started glowing as soon as I walked into her room. She lay on the bed with her eyes wide open." Dacia pulled her hand through her hair and shivered. "It was freaky. I decided I didn't need to see anything else, so

I turned to leave. There was a noise behind me. I spun around, and Cassandra was right there."

Samantha gasped.

"She was like a … a zombie." Dacia stared at a spot on the carpet. "She was reaching for my neck. She told me, 'There's no hope for you. My lord will take his rightful place in history. You will be destroyed.' She followed me around the room. Her movements were stiff, nothing like the way she normally is."

He should have talked her out of going. He should have kept her here. She needed somebody to help her make the right decisions, not to just go along with her.

"I told her to stop, and she did." Dacia squeezed Cody's fingers. "I asked why she was following me and what she wanted. She said, 'I want you dead. We all want you dead.'" Her face paled, and she looked into Sarah's eyes. "Then it was like my powers got sucked out of me. My chest tightened until my lungs burned. Everything went out of focus, and I barely made it through the door before she got hold of me."

The room stayed silent while everyone took in all that Dacia had said. Cody stared at a spot on the carpet, wondering why he had gone along, why he hadn't made her open the door and let him in.

Sarah was the first to speak. "Did she know what she was doing?"

"What difference does it make?" Cody spun around to face her, narrowing his eyes as he did.

Sarah returned his angry stare. "I want to know what's going on with her. She's not going to classes, and her friends think she's comatose."

"Bryce is a grade 'A' jerk"—Dacia clutched the necklace—"but the amulet hasn't shown any signs of life when I've seen him by himself. With Cassandra, it brightened her entire room."

"Thank you, Dacia," Sarah said, then leaned back in the desk chair. "I'm trying to get a handle on everything. You need to remember this is a new experience for me, too."

"Sorry." Cody lowered his gaze. He shouldn't have snapped at her. She didn't deserve it. "I'm edgy and overprotective."

"I understand." Sarah nodded. "However, you need to realize I'm not the enemy."

Samantha rubbed her arms. "What did you mean when you said you felt like you were being strangled? Was she strangling you?"

"No." Dacia sat quietly for a minute. "I felt like the air was being squeezed from my lungs, but Cassandra didn't lay a hand on me. The edges of my vision went black, and I panicked. That made things worse."

Samantha's shoulder dropped, and she tilted her head. "I wonder why Cassandra was able to make you quit breathing. Do you suppose she has some of Nefarious' powers?"

"I don't know." Dacia rubbed her hand over her forehead. "Nefarious hasn't ever made me quit breathing. I'm just not sure. Maybe I had an anxiety attack or something. I wish I knew what was going on."

"I think Samantha's onto something here." Sarah tapped her finger against her chin. "There have been times when you started to tell us about your dreams, and you said you felt like the wind was knocked out of you. Was that the same feeling?"

"Yeah, but more intense."

Cody felt like a hand had reached into his chest and clutched his heart. "Maybe she does then."

"Maybe. I don't need this. " She raked her fingers through her hair. "New subject. I'm going to try to make it to your office for my lesson this afternoon. You've been over here a lot, and there are more people over here to—"

"Yeah, I know what you mean," Sarah agreed. "If you can't make it, let me know, and please have Cody walk with you. Try to get some rest before our lesson," Sarah said as she walked to the door. "You need your strength."

Cody wrapped his arm around Dacia's waist, and they walked to Sarah's office. Well, technically he walked, and she hovered beside him, moving her feet to imitate walking. She had been somber since that morning's events, and Cody had no idea how to snap her out of it.

When they walked into Cacomistle Hall, Alicia was on the phone. She waved at them and pointed toward the stairs.

"I'm waiting for a call." Sarah met them at the door and led them to the couches. "Have a seat, and I'll be out in a couple of minutes."

Cody helped Dacia get as comfortable as she could. "Sure," he said to Sarah.

When he positioned himself next to Dacia, he noticed the vase sitting on the coffee table. It didn't belong in a room like this. It should have been behind glass in a museum or under lock and key. It was gold encrusted with precious gems.

Dacia reached forward but stopped and pointed at a leather pouch sitting beside it. "I wonder what that is."

"To carry it," Cody guessed as he leaned forward and studied it.

"Could be." She picked up the vase, and a sweet smile lifted her mouth.

The expression released the built-up tension inside of him. A weight seemed to fall off his chest, and he breathed easier. "You're smiling." Cody trailed his fingers over her lips. "Why?"

She closed her eyes at his touch. "I don't know. When I picked this up, things didn't seem so hopeless. It's almost like this vase has a spirit of its own, a very noble spirit. I know that sounds stupid, but I don't think somebody evil could touch it."

"Most things said in this room sound stupid but have a lot of truth to them." Cody lifted his hands. The last month or so had shown him that anything could happen. "I don't think I'll ever say something sounds stupid again."

"Yeah." She focused on the vase. "I know what you mean."

Noticing an inscription, Cody pointed at it. "What does it say?"

"Hope lives even in the darkest realms." She smiled again, and he wondered if the words alone gave her hope.

Sarah walked back into the room. "It's very intricate, isn't it?" She stared down at the vase. "I only wish I knew what it was for."

"Me too." Dacia peeled her gaze away from it long enough to glance at Sarah.

"Made you smile." Cody rubbed her shoulder. "Last few days you've been miserable. Nice to see you smile again."

Sarah looked Dacia over, and Cody's gaze followed hers. "You don't strike me as the type to be won over by pretty objects," Sarah said to her.

"No, not really." Dacia tucked her hands into her hoodie's pouch. "When I picked it up, I felt like maybe every cloud does have a silver lining … I guess I just need to search a little harder to find this one."

Sarah sat across from them. She propped her elbow on the arm of the couch and held her face. "That's a good outlook."

Dacia pulled the stopper out of the vase and peered into it. "Well, it obviously has some other purpose." She plugged it again, then seemed to notice the confusion on Sarah's and Cody's faces. "Oh, uh, there's no water in it, so it isn't a bottomless flask like the journal said."

"Interesting." Sarah's eyebrows pinched together. "Hopefully, we can figure something out."

"Maybe it was a bottomless flask because the hero needed it to be." Cody leaned forward and studied the vase. He wasn't sure where the thought had come from, but it seemed right. "You've been down, so it gave you hope."

Sarah tapped her finger on her cheek. "That's an interesting theory. It's possible it transforms into what's needed at the time. However, if you didn't know its properties changed, you might just toss it aside."

"Right now, I just need it to give me the answers to help me end this." Dacia held the vase, turning it over in her hands. "Can I take this with me? I'd like to see if I can figure it out."

Sarah nodded at the bag on the table. "Don't let other people see it. I like to believe people are good and honest, but I could see that sprouting legs and walking off. I'm sure it's worth a pretty penny."

"No problem." Dacia set the vase back down on the coffee table. "But, I think it's worth two or three pretty pennies or more than I will make in my entire lifetime."

Sarah looked at Cody. "Are you staying?"

"I'd like him to," Dacia said at the same time that he answered, "Yeah."

He leaned back, throwing his arm over the couch. He'd been ready to explain to Sarah why he needed to stay by Dacia's side. He'd been prepared to argue and fight for it if he had to, but with Dacia's answer, he let out a relieved breath.

Dacia lifted her injured leg onto the couch and leaned back against him. Then she stared out the window.

Cody rubbed his hand from her elbow to her shoulder. Touching her had become second nature to him. The action soothed him and seemed to relax her.

Dacia's voice was quiet when she said, "I think I'm going to have to face Nefarious soon."

"What makes you say that?" Sarah crossed one foot behind the other and leaned forward.

"Gut feeling. I think I can hold my own against him for a while, but in the end, he will win. I'm more powerful than I was, but …" She let her words trail off, but it was obvious there was more she wanted to say. "I don't know how to stop him. I barely know enough to keep myself alive. Nefarious knows several ways to kill me. I just can't quite figure out why he hasn't yet. It's like he's playing cat and mouse with me. One of these days, he'll pounce. And wham!" She slammed her hands together. "Everything will be over."

A nearly deafening silence filled the room. Cody slid his hand down Dacia's arm to her hand and twined his fingers through hers. This was all becoming too real. What had started as a far-fetched prophecy had moved into a full-blown threat. Dread crept up his spine. It wrapped its cold fingers around his heart and squeezed. He couldn't lose her, not now. He needed more time with her. He needed forever.

Sarah smoothed her tan slacks. "I believe Nefarious had to let your powers develop before fighting you."

Dacia shot up, pulling away from Cody. "Why?"

"I believe he has to fight a worthy opponent in order to rule the world." She folded her hands in her lap, calm as could be, like she told people every day that she was training them so they could die. "He could have killed you before, but it wouldn't have fulfilled the prophecy."

The icy fear that had held Cody in its clutches moments before disappeared. It was replaced by an inferno burning within him. Heat flared through his body. He clenched his jaw and felt all of his muscles tighten.

Sparks flickered on Dacia's fingertips. She clenched her hands and breathed in deeply. "Why did you let me learn? Why didn't you just leave me alone?"

"I can see where this doesn't make a lot of sense." Sarah held her hands up like she was surrendering.

"It doesn't make a lot of sense? It doesn't make any sense!" Dacia's voice rose.

Cody couldn't remember ever seeing Dacia like this before. Her body shook. Her breath whooshed in and out like she'd just finished a marathon. He could see her pulse pounding in her neck, and he was afraid that her power would surge out of her, risking everyone in the building. Flames still danced on her fingertips, so he held onto her wrist. With his thumb, he gently rubbed the back of her hand.

The flames extinguished. Dacia's breaths slowed, and her tremors stilled.

Sarah watched, waiting to speak until Dacia had calmed down. "If I'd left you alone, he would've killed you and taken his chances with whatever came next. It's not like there are very many people out there who could challenge him. I wanted you to have a chance."

"A chance?" Dacia's voice was high-pitched.

Sarah pushed her sleeve up as far as its buttoned cuff would allow. "I should have said something to you earlier. I'm sorry."

"Yeah." Dacia let a breath out through her teeth.

Cody could understand why Dacia was so upset. If he was in her position, he probably would be too, but he could also see why Sarah had wanted to train her. Since coming to Phlox University, Dacia's powers and her control had increased dramatically. Before coming here, she wouldn't have stood a chance against Nefarious, but now … well he didn't know if she did, but she was closer.

Since his touch seemed to soothe her, he continued tracing circles on her hand. "If Nefarious attacked before, you'd've died. Training was for the best."

"Whatever." She swiped at her eyes, trying to stop her tears from falling.

"I'm sorry, Dacia." Sarah ran her hand over her face. "I should've told you."

Dacia crossed her arms over her chest and glared at Sarah. "You think?"

"I didn't." Sarah pinned her with a look. "You already thought I was nuts when I told you about the prophecy. If I'd have told you then, you wouldn't have come back into my office ever again."

"Maybe I shouldn't have!" On the shelves, the books rattled nervously. "I'm sorry that I don't like being sacrificed!"

Sarah stood in front of Dacia, pointing her finger down at her, and Cody had to commend her bravery. "I am not sacrificing you! I'm trying to help you save your life and the lives of everyone else on this miserable planet. If you can't see that, I'm sorry! I wanted you to stand against Nefarious and fight, not cower in some corner while he destroyed you. I guess I assumed you would want a chance."

Cody kept his mouth shut. This was between the two of them. He resituated himself on the couch, trying to find a more comfortable position. Dacia stared at her lap or at the floor; he couldn't tell for sure which. Sarah stood in front of them with her arms folded.

Finally, Dacia swallowed. "Sorry." Her voice was small, but the word filled the uncomfortable silence, drowning it out.

"Me too," Sarah said.

Chapter 21

Too Close For Comfort

$\mathcal{D}$acia sat on Cody's lap. Her head leaned against his shoulder, and her legs were draped over the arm of the chair. He was careful not to jostle her injury.

Between her nightmares and his worry, he hadn't gotten a lot of sleep lately, but exhaustion weighed him down more than he thought it should. He fought against his third yawn in mere minutes, holding it in until it erupted from within him. "Sorry. I'm beat."

"I think that might be my fault." She lifted her head and acted like she was about to get up. "I thought you might be able to help me heal."

"Then use me." He wrapped his arms around her so she couldn't get away.

"No, I didn't know it would hurt you."

Samantha flipped through the channels, not finding anything worth watching. "What if you used some of his energy, then tried to use some of mine?"

"I already used some of his." She moved so that none of her skin came in contact with his. "We'll see how he's doing in the morning."

Samantha stopped on the local news. "A winter storm is approaching," the weatherman predicted. "We could see up to twenty inches of snow in some areas over a two-day period."

Dacia slumped back a little.

"We'll have more on this as the storm approaches. Stay tuned to Channel 5 for 'The Most Accurate Weather in the Area'."

"Awesome! I love snow." Cody smiled at Dacia, but it faded when he saw her expression.

She was as pale as a ghost. "No, no, no."

"Are you okay?" Samantha asked before he had the chance.

Dacia shook her head slowly as if she were in denial. "I'm terrified. All of my nightmares have been snowy lately." She latched onto Cody's hand, squeezing his fingers until he felt his bones pressing together.

He pried his fingers free and wiggled them, getting the blood flowing back through them again.

"Sorry." She lifted her lips in a sheepish grin. "I'm not ready, and I have no idea what to do."

Samantha set the remote down. "Well, if this storm hits before next weekend, I doubt I'll be going home. I know it's not much, but I can offer you moral support."

"Yeah." They sat in silence for a moment before Dacia said, "Let's not dwell on this right now; it's not like weathermen are always right. Pick out a movie so we can get our minds on something else. Something funny would be nice."

Trying to figure out what she was thinking, he looked at her through the corner of his eyes. There was no way she'd moved on from her dread that quickly, but was she planning something or just trying to comfort them?

Footsteps woke Cody up. He immediately looked at Cookie Monster, but Dacia wasn't there. He jumped up and saw her by the door. "Where you going?" He stretched his arms above his head, and the movement lifted his shirt up. He noticed when Dacia's gaze slid to the exposed skin there, and he couldn't deny that he liked the way she looked at him and the heat that turned her cheeks rosy.

"To check out my leg. I think it finally healed! Look at me. I'm standing here." She motioned with both hands to emphasize her journey from the chair. "I walked here!"

"That's great, Dacia." He strode toward her and put his hands on her shoulders, waiting until she looked him in the eyes. "Please, come right back."

"I will." She sashayed out of the room, and Cody prayed that she would keep her word.

While she was gone, he paced the floor like a restless tiger. Back and forth. Back and forth. Staring at the door, waiting for Dacia to walk back through it.

"Well?" Cody asked as soon as she stepped inside.

She covered her lips with a finger and pointed toward Samantha's loft. "Let's go somewhere else to talk."

He grabbed her hand, and the two of them went outside.

Usually, Dacia lifted her face to the sky and let the fresh air invigorate her. As soon as they stepped through the doors, her shoulders slumped, and her excitement dissipated. "I'm going to class. I'm sick of sitting around with nothing on my mind but Nefarious."

"Your leg's better then?"

She pulled her pant leg up. An enormous scar covered her skin, but it had healed. His gaze traveled over the injury, then met hers. "Wow." He squeezed her hand. "I thought it'd be worse."

"Worse?" She shook her head and looked at him like he was speaking a foreign language. "I'll never be able to let anyone see it."

"Why?" Still holding her hand, he strode toward a bench and sat on it. She plopped down next to him, and he wrapped his arm around her. "Yesterday, it was gruesome. Today it's a scar. Maybe tomorrow it'll be a memory."

She threw her legs over his and scooted until she could lay her head against his chest. "How are you feeling? Did I take too much?"

"Fine." He traced her ear with his finger. "I slept like a log." He slid his hand down her side to pull her closer still. His knuckles collided with the leather pouch hanging from her belt loop. He hadn't noticed that she'd grabbed it this morning. "Did you figure it out?"

"No, but I think I should keep it with me." She nuzzled in closer to him. "It has to serve some purpose. But if it's not with me, I won't have it when I need it."

"Makes sense." He drew his finger down her neck, then lifted her chin. "Everything okay? You seem down. Thought you'd be happy since your leg's better."

"I was ecstatic. It felt great to walk around on my own, but when I was in the shower, I thought about my dream with Nefarious. In it, my leg was healed." Her chin trembled, and unshed tears glistened in her eyes. "I don't want it to be better before this weekend."

"You don't know it's this weekend." He brushed his thumb along her jaw. "You know it snowed and your leg had healed. You don't know if it's this weekend or next year."

"You're right." She stared off into the distance, and Cody was certain she didn't believe what she was saying. "I'm not sure it's this weekend."

"Let's leave." He didn't know why he hadn't thought of it before. It was so simple. If Nefarious didn't know where she was, he couldn't come after her. His time on Earth would end, and Dacia would be free.

"What?"

Cody dropped his hand. "Let's go away before the storm hits."

She sat up, pulling away from him. "And lead Nefarious to our homes and families." She dropped her head. "No. I can't take that chance."

"Don't have to go home." He wasn't ready to give up on this idea yet.

She looked up at him, and the sadness in her eyes broke his heart. "He knew I was here. He'll know how to find me. Somehow, he'll know. I can feel it."

Cody held her close. His hand traveled the length of her spine, up, then down, soothing, comforting. He'd thought he'd found the answer, but now, they were back at square one. "I know you can't see it, but it'll work out."

"I know what the light at the end of the tunnel is, Cody. It's the pearly gates, and I'm not ready to see them yet." Her tone was cold and emotionless.

"Have a little faith."

"I do. If I didn't, how would I find myself standing at the pearly gates when this is all said and done? You don't end up there without faith." She leaned her head back and looked into his eyes.

He stood up, setting her down on the ground next to him. "Please don't give up."

"I won't." She wrapped her arm around his waist, tucking her hand into his back pocket. "But the odds are against me."

"Still going to class?"

"Yeah, I should." She inhaled deeply and straightened her shoulders. "I better keep my grades up in case you're right."

Cody couldn't do much against monsters and magic, but he could walk with Dacia to class. Maybe not seeing her alone would diminish the chance of an attack against her. Besides, he relished any opportunity to spend time with her.

When he stepped into the classroom and saw Bryce, Alvin, and Vanessa sitting there, he decided to walk her to her desk.

"Watch your back," Bryce said when they walked past him.

Cody clenched his fist but otherwise didn't react. He hoped, that with as quiet as Bryce had said it, Dacia didn't notice.

She looked over her shoulder, and Cody realized she had. She turned back around and clutched his jacket, limping the rest of the way to her chair.

"You okay?" He knelt beside her, careful not to touch her and somehow hurt her more.

Her breaths tore from her lungs, ragged and broken. "My leg feels like it's on fire again."

"You need to leave?" *Please.*

She shook her head, and when she looked at him, fear and pain darkened her emerald eyes. "No, I'm okay. I just hope it's not injured again. I don't think I can handle that." Her face relaxed a little, and her breathing normalized. "Nefarious must be controlling one of them." She lifted the chain, keeping the amulet under her shirt and out of sight.

Cody rubbed his forehead. He didn't want to leave her alone with them. She was just beginning to heal. "They're all possessed." *Come with me*, he wanted to beg, but he knew she wouldn't.

"Go to your class, Cody." She squeezed his shoulder and shot him a smile. It wasn't reassuring. "I'll be fine."

Cody meant to go to his class, but when he walked past them on his way out, he remembered what they had done to him. He remembered the satisfaction they'd gotten out of beating him.

He knew Dacia wouldn't like it, but he waited in the hallway, out of her sight, and kept an eye on them. As soon as class ended, he walked to Dacia's seat and helped her up. When he was sure that she could stand on her own, he put his hand in the middle of her back and guided her past Bryce, Vanessa, and Alvin.

Once they were in the hallway, she narrowed her eyes at him. "You skipped."

"Was worried." He tugged one of her curls, watching it spring back into place when he let go. "Didn't like the looks they gave you."

She rolled her eyes at him, but he didn't care. Right now, she was safe, and he would do whatever it took to keep her that way. He silently wished he could stay with her until English Lit started, but he had a test.

He walked her to the empty classroom, and his stomach sank. If something happened here, there would be no witnesses, but Dacia had insisted. He took one more look around, making sure nobody else was there. "I'm late." He gave her a quick goodbye peck. "Stay here."

"I know you've heard it before, but I will." She sat at her usual desk and started pulling out books from her backpack. When he didn't leave right away, she shooed him off like he was a pesky fly.

Cody sat through his American History class staring at the monitor. *Watch your back.* The screen might as well have been blank for all that he saw on it. *Watch your back.* Bryce's words ran through his head over and over again. *Watch your back.*

He needed to pass this test. He knew the answers. He'd known them most of his life, but he couldn't even focus on the questions. He could just see Bryce's smug face and hear his words. *Watch your back.*

The way he'd said it had made it sound like he was asking her to be careful and not threatening her, but why would he suddenly turn into a decent human instead of a cretin?

Cody wiped his hands down his face and read the question for the fourth time. "Which of the following was NOT a reason for the United States' entry into WWI?" He selected a random answer and moved on, deciding it was better to answer them all and hope to get a few right than to leave them all blank.

As soon as class was over, he darted out of the room, squeezing between people, and practically sprinted to Quartz Building. The closer he got, the more he felt that something terrible had happened. The hair on his arms and on the back of his neck rose like a balloon had been rubbed over them.

"Let her be okay," he repeated under his breath.

He pushed the door to the classroom open and stared. Dacia sat slumped over her desk, and blood dripped off of her hair onto her paper.

He couldn't see any signs of a struggle. *She musta fallen asleep.* He reached for her arm, realizing how vulnerable she'd been. If Nefarious or one of the Potato Heads had found her like this, what would they have done to her?

"Dacia." His voice caught, making her name wobble. He knelt next to her desk.

"Dacia." He tried to ignore the students surrounding him. "Dacia." When she didn't respond, he shook her shoulders. "Dacia, please wake up." Emotion choked his voice.

Her eyes fluttered open. She squinted at him and slowly lifted her head. She didn't make it very far before slumping forward again.

Sick of listening to the whispers, Cody lifted her, pressing her body close to his, and carried her past the gawkers. She hung limply in his arms. Her open eyes seemed to take in everything around her.

Bryce stood by the door. He clutched the strap of his backpack with one hand and had his other tucked into his pocket. His pale green gaze followed them, unnerving Cody. He couldn't recall ever seeing another person with eyes that color.

"I warned you." Bryce dragged his hand down his face. "I wish you'd have listened."

Cody tensed. Now was not the time to have it out with Bryce. He needed to get Dacia back to her room, to make sure she would be okay, and to figure out what had happened.

He raced to the dorm, careful not to jog her too much. Her eyes had rolled back in her head and seeing the whites staring up at him freaked him out. Fortunately, somebody was leaving Wisteria Hall as he arrived. She held the door open for him, and he hurried up the three flights of steps to Dacia's room.

He kicked the door with his foot, hoping Samantha was still inside.

"Just a minute." She sounded like she was talking through a yawn.

"Can't wait, Sam." Cody's voice sounded frantic even to him. "*Hurry!*"

"Just hold your horses, Cody." He heard a thud and assumed Samantha had jumped when she reached the last couple of steps of the ladder like he'd seen her do before. "I was still sleeping. You have a …" Her voice trailed off when she opened the door and saw Cody holding Dacia.

"Know I have a key"—even though Dacia was light, carrying her that far while running had taxed his muscles—"but couldn't reach it." He carried Dacia inside, careful not to bump her against the doorframe, then laid her on the floor.

A broken doll.

Chapter 22

Scarier Than Hell

Cody stood with Sarah and Samantha between the door and the computer. They were talking softly, but he really wasn't paying attention. He was too focused on Dacia. *Why isn't she waking up?* he thought for the millionth time.

"If she doesn't wake up soon, we're going to have to take her to the hospital," Sarah said. The look on her face left no room for argument, but Cody would do everything in his power to keep it from happening.

He knew Dacia wouldn't want that. What if they did tests and found out she was different? What would they do to her then? He turned away from her, scrubbing his hand down his face, trying to find the words to say to make Sarah understand why they couldn't betray Dacia like that.

"Wha … happed … to … me?" Dacia whispered.

Cody's mouth went dry as he rushed over. "Dacia." His words trembled. "Thank God."

"Wa'er." Her voice was gravelly, but she was awake. She was talking.

"Sure, I'll get it." Samantha headed toward the fridge, looking relieved to be doing something other than standing and waiting.

When she brought the water over, Dacia struggled to lift herself onto her elbows. They wobbled, and she fell back.

Cody was there immediately. He cradled her head, lifting it enough so she could drink. Then with his other hand, he brought the bottle to her lips, tipping it too much. Water poured down her chin onto her shirt.

"Sorry." Heat erupted on Cody's neck, rising up onto his cheeks. "I didn't—"

"Iss kay," she mumbled. Her eyes rolled back, and she pressed them closed.

Cody felt her swaying and wondered if she was about to pass out again.

"Let's try sitting her up in one of the chairs." Sarah strode over like she was going to help Cody lift Dacia.

Cody waved her off, then slid his arms under Dacia, hoping not to hurt her. He slowly stood and eased his way to Cookie Monster. The chair rocked back as he sat, and he winced. Looking down, it didn't seem like it had affected Dacia one way or the other.

She resituated herself on his lap, and he wrapped his arms around her. He ran his hand up and down her arm and stared at her head nestled against his chest. She was here. She was safe for now.

He bent down and whispered right into her ear, "Take my energy. Heal yourself."

"Can't." She barely shook her head. "Might hurt you."

Tears burned his eyes, but he refused to let them fall in front of Sarah and Samantha. He hated that she was injured. He could help her if she would just let him. "Please, Dacia."

"Would you like to try another drink?" Sarah asked.

She nodded and rolled away from him.

With Sarah's help, Dacia ended up with more water in her mouth than on her clothes. Cody made a mental note not to switch his major to anything that had to do with taking care of people.

Samantha pulled out the desk chair and basically crumpled into it. He understood her actions completely because he felt the same. "You had us pretty scared."

"Dacia"—Sarah twisted the lid back on the bottle, then settled herself in Big Bird—"do you know what happened?"

In response, Dacia reached her hand up and tentatively touched the back of her head in several places. Then she stared at the pillow on the floor. Blood coated the case.

She pressed her eyes closed, and her chin dropped slightly toward her chest as if in defeat. "More water first."

Sarah pressed her hands down on the arms of the chair, but Dacia reached her hand out. "I'll do it."

Dacia's hand shook as she lifted the bottle to her mouth. She drank slowly, still looking at the pillow over the top of the bottle. "I promised Cody I'd wait for him, and I did. I was working on my homework when the power went out."

"Dacia, dear," Sarah said, "the power didn't go out on campus today."

"Whatever." From her tone, it was fairly clear that she didn't agree with Sarah. "The lights were out in …" Her eyes widened. "Oh … a dream."

"Figured so." At some point, Cody had gone back to tracing shapes on her arm. He didn't know if the action soothed Dacia, but it calmed him.

"Why?" She looked into his eyes as if the answers might be there.

The heaviness of everyone's stares made him squirm. "You were slumped over, bleeding."

She rubbed his side, and her touch reminded him that she was okay. She was here with him, in his arms.

"You wouldn't wake up. You didn't move." He brushed his hand across his eyes. "Carried you here, but you lost consciousness again. Samantha and I didn't think you were breathing …" His voice trailed off, and he wiped his eyes again. "Thought I lost you." He pulled her closer. *She's here. She's safe,* he reminded himself, but the annoying voice in his head asked, *For how long, though?*

She cupped his cheek in her hand and whispered, "I'm here."

"I can't …" He shook his head. "I can't lose you." He stared into her eyes while he composed himself. "It had to be a dream. If it wasn't, Nefarious would've ki—" his voice broke, and he cleared his throat "—finished you off."

She wrapped her arms around him as much as she could while sitting in the chair on his lap. "I'm okay."

Cody held onto her, hoping she couldn't feel his hands trembling. He needed to be strong for her. He needed her to know that he believed in her and that he would be there for her no matter what.

"The lights flickered, then died. The amulet flared, burning my skin." Dacia didn't look at any of them. She clutched Cody's t-shirt. "I saw his eyes. They glowed." She swallowed, then let go of his shirt before clasping it again. "Somehow, I was tied to the chair. The more I struggled, the tighter the ropes became.

"I couldn't get out. I tried to teleport back here." She looked up at them for just a second before turning away again. "I didn't want him to find me, so I turned invisible. He started throwing the chairs and eventually, threw mine. My head hit the wall, then nothing."

She pulled her hand through her hair, stopping when she reached the matted strands. "That's all I remember. I don't remember Cody carrying me or any of that … maybe with time. I would much rather remember my knight in shining armor coming to my rescue than the horrific beast trying to kill me."

Sarah leaned forward in her chair and tapped her finger against her chin. "That's understandable."

"How are you feeling now, Dacia?" At some point, Samantha had rolled her chair closer to them, but Cody hadn't noticed.

Dacia rubbed her forehead. "Stronger than when I first woke up. I think I might even be able to move on my own now."

"Great," Sarah said. "We didn't know how your body would handle any new injuries—if you would heal right away or if it would be more like your leg."

"I think my leg took longer to heal because that actually happened to me, so since my leg is getting better … if that is the case … I think my head will heal faster."

"Take my strength," Cody begged.

She lifted her hand to his face, brushing her thumb along his eye socket. "No. I'm getting better on my own." She scrunched her nose up. "I need to wash my hair. The smell is making me nauseous."

"I can help you with your hair if you need me to." Samantha went to her closet and pulled out a dark purple towel.

Sarah glanced at her watch. "If you're helping her, I'll excuse myself."

As soon as Sarah left, Dacia stood. She held onto the arms of the chair, making sure she was steady. Cody was ready to catch her in case she fell. She slowly straightened and waited a few seconds before she turned around. "I think I'll wash it here in our sink. That way I don't have to walk down the hall like this. I'm sure I've been the subject of enough conversations for one day."

"Yeah." Cody rubbed his neck, remembering the group of people he'd had to fight through to get to her and then to get her out. "People were talking before I made it to the door."

She snapped her head back. "Bryce was there, wasn't he?"

"Yeah." The fire that had burned inside of Cody since the Potato Heads had attacked him rose up as if a strong wind had stirred the embers, breathing life back into them. *Had he done this to her somehow?* "Why?"

"I think I remember him saying something when you carried me out." She rubbed her temples and squinted. "When you made that comment about people talking, it started to come back to me."

Cody's breath roared in his ears. His eyes narrowed, and he clenched and unclenched his fists. There was no way he would ever be able to forgive Bryce for any of this. "He said he warned you to watch your back."

"But why?" Dacia glanced around, rubbing the back of her neck.

Cody's voice was hard. "Wanted to gloat."

"Gloat about what? He didn't make me fall asleep or give me nightmares. It doesn't make sense." She wiped her hands over her face and looked from Samantha to Cody. "My head's still foggy. I'm probably not thinking right."

Samantha washed Dacia's hair while Dacia clung to the sides of the sink. When she was lathering Dacia's hair for the third time, she said, "Oh, I forgot. The body shop called. Your truck will be ready for you to pick up tomorrow."

"Thanks." Cody noticed her knuckles whiten as she held on tighter to the porcelain.

He was surprised that she hadn't sounded a little more excited about it. He wasn't sure he wanted her to have it again. It was hard enough to keep her from sneaking out without a vehicle, but he thought she would be happy.

Chapter 23

Cowboy Up

"Dacia." Cody stood on her ladder and shook her shoulder. This was the first time she'd slept in her bed since she was attacked by Nefarious. "You're late."

She pulled the blanket over her head and rolled onto her side.

The action made him chuckle. She wasn't a morning person, and he found her all the cuter for it. "Skipping class?" He wouldn't blame her if she did.

"You should go." Samantha rinsed her toothbrush off and put it back in its holder. "You missed Tuesday."

"Just five more minutes." She sounded like a little kid, begging her mom.

"If you're going, you need to get up." Cody started to back down the ladder. "Class starts in twenty minutes."

Grudgingly, she pulled the blanket back and sat up. Cody waited, hoping she would let him help her down. When she did, he had to fight to hide his surprise.

Dacia brushed her teeth, pulled her hair into a ponytail, and tugged a hoodie on over her pajamas.

Cody tried to grab her backpack before she could, but she snagged it out from under his hand. She seemed to be steady on her feet this morning, but he was afraid it wouldn't last.

He held her hand as they strolled to Algebra. Not wanting to strain her, he tried to keep an easy pace, but he was on edge. Too many things had happened lately. Too many things had gone wrong to assume that they would be okay today. "Althea after class? We can eat lunch. Then I'll take you to pick up your truck."

"Really?" She snapped her head back and stopped walking. "You want to take me to get my truck?"

"Yeah, that's what he said." Samantha tapped her foot against the sidewalk. They were pushing making it to class on time, and that was one of her biggest pet peeves. "I can drive one of them if you don't want to."

"Oh, wow. I, uh"—Dacia pulled her fingers through her hair—"I didn't think anybody would want me to have it. I thought you'd be scared I'd take off again."

Cody shrugged and started walking. "Well, if you don't want it—"

"No. I want it." She grasped her backpack strap and hoisted it up onto her shoulder. "I didn't think I'd ever see my baby again."

"What do you mean by that?" Samantha fell into step beside them.

"I didn't think you guys would take me to pick it up until after the prophecy's taken care of—" she fidgeted with the shoulder straps, not looking at either of them "—and I don't think I'll be around after that."

Cody closed his eyes and pulled his hand down his face. She'd been his best friend since second grade, and now, she was his life. He couldn't imagine her not being there anymore. He needed her to get through this. "Please, stop talking like that."

"Sorry, Cody. I'm trying to prepare you." She kicked a rock as they walked along. "I'm not going to win."

Samantha stopped and planted her hands on her hips. "Dacia, Cody's right. You have to stop thinking like that, or you won't walk away from this. You need to have faith in yourself. Instead of giving up, maybe you should do something to figure out how to defeat him."

"Like what?" she asked, flinging her hands into the air. "I've been going to lessons, reading the journals over and over again, and trying to figure out what to do, what the vase is for. What else am I supposed to do?" She yanked a shaking hand through her hair, looking like she was on the verge of tears. "If you have any ideas, I'd love to hear them."

"Why don't we search some mythology books?" Samantha tugged on her bottom lip. Several other students walked by, and when she spoke again, her voice was significantly quieter. "There may be a solution buried in one. Now that we've seen fairies and know of the existence of other magical creatures, I wonder if some of those books are nonfiction."

"It's worth a try." Dacia lifted a shoulder, and Cody thought something like hope might have sparked in her eyes. "When we get back from Althea, maybe we can go to the library."

"I have class this afternoon," Samantha said. "But after …"

"I'll go with you." Cody walked alongside Dacia and rubbed her neck. Her muscles were hardened from tension. "Maybe something will give you hope. I hate seeing you so defeated."

Dacia's leg bounced up and down throughout class. At one point, she even reached down and squeezed Cody's knee, eliciting an amused smile from him. He hadn't seen her this excited in quite a while.

As soon as class was over, the three of them went straight to Cody's car. "The Avalanche first." He started the ignition, then turned the radio down. "After we eat, we'll get your truck. Then we won't have two vehicles the whole time. Okay?"

"Fine by me." Dacia pulled her seatbelt across her body and snapped it into place. "How about you, Sam?"

"Yeah, sounds good. Cody's driving. He's the boss. Besides, when hasn't he wanted food first?"

"Ouch." He pretended to be hurt by the comment, but he was just glad that Dacia was in better spirits. "Be nice."

Cody pulled out of the parking lot. One hand held the steering wheel, and one held Dacia's. Her fingers were soft and warm, delicate compared to his. And, though they had been holding hands on occasion for years, there was something different about this. It wasn't just about being friends or needing comfort. It was letting her know that he loved her, that he was there for her and would always be.

She pulled her hand away, grabbed the dash, and gasped. Then she bent over clutching her neck, sucking in breaths that didn't fill her lungs.

"Dacia"—Samantha's voice was high and fast—"are you okay?"

Cody pulled onto the shoulder and slammed the car into park. He reached over and rubbed Dacia's back. "Breathe." His voice was soft, soothing. "You're okay." He looked around, trying to figure out what had happened, and realized they were just beyond where she had wrecked.

She kept her head bowed. "It seems like an eternity ago, but when we drove by, it felt like it was happening again."

Cody slid his hand down her arm. He had no idea what she was going through. He didn't know if it had something to do with the demon or if it was some form of PTSD, but he wanted to be there for her. He waited for her breathing to even out, then asked, "Okay now?"

Dacia nodded and sat up, staring out the window. "You can go."

The rest of the drive was tense. Samantha's gaze met Cody's in the rearview mirror, and she mouthed, "Is she okay?"

Cody glanced at Dacia. Her muscles were tense, and her hands were clenched in tight fists in her lap.

He lifted his shoulder toward his ear and shook his head. Was she okay? Would she ever be?

Cody parked on the street in front of The Avalanche. He held Dacia's hand as they walked in. They sat in a booth. Dacia snuggled up to Cody, and Samantha sat across from them.

When they finished eating, they went to Sycamore's Auto Repair. Dacia's truck was pulled up right in front of the door. The black paint shone in the sunlight. As soon as Cody came to a stop, Dacia hopped out.

Cody got out and leaned against his car, watching Dacia but hanging back. She peered through the driver's window for several seconds, then shook her head before walking inside the building.

When she came back out, she handed Samantha her keys. "Will you drive it back?"

"Are you sure, Dacia?" Samantha's eyebrows furrowed in confusion.

"Yeah." Dacia dragged her hand through her hair. "I don't want to drive right now."

Samantha looked at the keys, dangling from Dacia's fingers. "But you were so excited."

Dacia sighed. "I know. I'm afraid to drive it. Too many things have happened lately." She ran her hand over the hood. "At least it'll be back on campus in case I need it."

"Are you sure you don't want to drive it?" Samantha finally took the keys, looking at them like they might bite her. "I'll ride back with you."

Dacia shook her head.

"Why not?" Cody hooked his thumbs in his belt loops. "Cowboy up. Don't get behind the wheel, you never will."

She snatched her keys from Samantha and climbed in. Clenching her hands on the wheel, she waited for Samantha to get in. Tears welled up in her eyes.

Cody leaned through the window. "I'll follow you. Be careful."

Dacia drove slower than Cody usually did. Her truck didn't hug the curves on the mountain roads like his car did. *And, she's scared of driving now,* he reminded himself.

Cody pulled into the parking lot next to Dacia. He walked around his car to her door, and when she stepped out, he said, "You did fine."

Samantha swatted him with the back of her hand. "Cody, Dacia isn't afraid of driving. She's afraid of driving with Nefarious on the loose. And if we were in her position, we would be, too." She turned toward Dacia. "Now I've got to get to class, but I'll help you research later."

"Okay, thanks."

"Sorry." Cody slid his hand over Dacia's, slipping his fingers between hers. "Thought you were scared."

"Don't worry about it. It's water under the bridge." She rubbed her thumb over his. "Should we go to the library now?"

"Yeah, let's see what we can find."

They sat at a table in the corner surrounded by stacks of mythology books, flipping through pages, hoping for a miracle. Book after book was thrown onto the return pile.

"Find anything?" Samantha asked as she pulled out a chair next to them.

"No," they both replied.

At 9:50, Dacia slammed the last book in her stack closed and leaned back, pulling her hand through her hair. "In all of the books I have looked through, I haven't found anything helpful about defeating demons, but I learned tons about jinni, some fascinating stuff actually. I also read about unicorns, Pegasus, manticores, and oodles of other creatures. Either nobody has ever defeated a Balor demon without a magical sword, or nobody has recorded it."

"I didn't find anything in any of these books either." Cody waved his hand at a stack on the floor beside him. "What about you, Sam?"

"Nothing. I've gone cross-eyed from staring at these." She gathered her books together. "We should get going."

Cody sat quietly for a moment. "The last champion defeated Nefarious, so it had to have been recorded."

"Right," Dacia agreed.

"You'd think one of his friends would've written something about him, made him into a hero or a god. You'd think they'd have tried to immortalize him somehow," Samantha said, finishing Cody's thought.

"Maybe a ballad," Cody said.

"Nefarious probably destroyed his friends." Dacia stood and stacked her books onto a cart. "He's tried to get mine, and this isn't over yet."

"Don't remind me." Samantha shuddered. "He's tried with Cody and Sarah … I keep wondering when it will be my turn."

Chapter 24

Skipping

Cody walked Dacia to her Speech class. As soon as they stepped inside, heads turned in their direction. People gathered in groups and whispered to each other. Their gazes followed Dacia and Cody across the room.

Dacia seemed to shrink in on herself. She lowered her head and slunk to her desk.

Cody tried to hear what was being said, but the hushed words blurred into a hum. He pressed his hand to the small of her back, hoping to give her some comfort. "You okay?"

"Fine."

He was surprised by the venom in her voice, but he couldn't blame her for it. He stood next to her desk, wondering if he should leave. He looked over his shoulder at the door, and she grabbed his hand.

"Just hurry back after your class. If I'm alone, it'll be easier for everyone to pester me."

"I will." He gave her a quick kiss, wanting to draw it out, but not wanting to draw more attention to her.

With every step he took away from her, he fought the urge to turn around and drag her out of that room. She didn't need to be alone with the rumors and the gossip. She didn't need everyone's focus on her. He knew what that could do to her control. He'd seen it firsthand.

But she hadn't asked him to stay. She needed him to show her that he had faith in her. Her hope was fading fast, and he had to prove that he trusted her.

He went to class, but he snuck out a few minutes early and ran back to Quartz Building, hoping to save Dacia from too many questions. He walked into the room and spotted Dacia near her desk. Two girls he'd never seen around her before were pestering her. He wanted to tell them to leave her alone, but instead, he flashed a charming smile at them. "Excuse us. We have to get to class." He grabbed Dacia's elbow and led her out.

They walked outside, dodging questions and ignoring stares. As soon as they stepped through the door, Cody led her around the corner of the building and backed her up against the wall. "If you want to skip, we can." He braced his hands against the stones, one on either side of her shoulders. "Maybe by Monday, Wednesday will be forgotten."

She flattened her palms on his chest. He hadn't expected it, and the action sent a flood of emotion through him. He closed his eyes and sucked in a breath.

"That's the best thing I've heard in a long time." She stepped closer, and he wrapped his arms around her. With her head leaning against his chest, she said, "I haven't set anybody's books on fire for a while, and that's the last thing I need today."

Cody slid his arm down to her waist and turned her toward the dorms. "Beautiful day. Might be last one for a while. Wanna go to the lake?"

"A change of scenery would be nice." Her shoulders relaxed.

They walked behind the dorm, taking the path toward Falcon Lake. The sun shone through the trees, making shadows dance across their bodies.

"Could you do me a favor?" Dacia looked up at him, and he knew he would never be able to deny her anything no matter how badly he wanted to.

He smiled at her, hoping she wouldn't ask for something he would regret giving to her. "Anything."

"Let's not talk about the weather today."

He squeezed her fingers. "Sure, Dacia."

They stepped out of the trees, and Falcon Lake spread out in front of them with the Snowfire Mountains reflecting across the surface of the water. The sun highlighted their frosted peaks. The air smelled cleaner here, fresh and pine-scented. It wasn't far from campus, but it felt worlds away.

Dacia and Cody strolled along in comfortable silence. When they reached the playground, Dacia said, "Let's swing. I haven't done that for so long."

She sat on the plastic seat, gripped the chains, swayed from side to side, and stared at the scenery like she wanted to disappear in it. "I love it here. The mountains are so peaceful, beautiful."

"Yeah, they are." After several more minutes, Cody jumped off his swing and stretched his hand toward Dacia.

She reluctantly grabbed hold of it. He wrapped his arm around her waist, and they walked to Sarah's office so Dacia could get to her lesson on time.

"Hello, Dacia, Cody." Sarah turned her back on them and walked to the couches. "How are you doing today?"

"Better after skipping." Dacia stood with her hands tucked into her hoodie's pouch.

"Skipping?" Sarah turned back. Her hazel eyes filled with concern as she looked Dacia over from head to toe. "You're not injured again, are you?"

"No." Dacia shook her head and pulled her hand through her windblown curls. "I wasn't coping, so Cody took me to Falcon Lake."

Sarah's lips pinched together. "It was a beautiful day for it, but your studies need to be a priority."

Cody stood next to Dacia, tracing a pattern on her arm. Sarah should have understood that Dacia needed a break, but he decided to stay out of this. He wanted Dacia to see that he believed she could handle herself.

"Have a seat." Sarah pointed at the couch without saying anything else.

"Well … actually, we were thinking about going to the library." Dacia looked from Sarah to Cody and back again. Then she told Sarah about Samantha's theory.

"Are there more books?"

Cody thought about the shelves in the library and all the books they hadn't had a chance to go through yet. "Yes, tons."

"Maybe your time would be better spent there. I can arrange for the library to stay open late for you." Sarah smoothed the creases in her slacks. "Are you okay, Dacia?"

Dacia leaned on the back of the couch and held her head in her hands. "I don't think it was supposed to be me. I don't know what I'm doing."

Sarah set her jaw. "This is a battle you can win."

"I—"

Sarah stuck her hand up, stopping Dacia's rebuttal. "Let me say what I have to say. Nefarious is evil, cruel, and monstrous. You are good, compassionate, and loyal. Perfect to defeat him. Who better to stop him than his exact opposite? Where he has hate, you have love. Where he has arrogance, you have humbleness. You just need a little faith."

Dacia looked down at her shoes. "I'm trying."

"Good then." Sarah smiled at Dacia, and in that look, Cody could see that Sarah believed everything she'd said. "Go find out how to defeat him."

Cody didn't press Dacia to walk any faster than she wanted to on their way to the library. They sauntered down the sidewalks, and she lifted her face to the sky, closing her eyes, and breathing deeply. "Do you ever think about how fate brought you here … where Sarah could help you?"

"Not for a while"—she shook her head—"but I guess someone was watching out for me. If I hadn't met Sarah, I doubt I would've lasted this long. Maybe you and Sarah are right. Maybe I just need some faith." Her lips parted slightly.

Cody draped his arm over her shoulders, pulling her against his side, and she wrapped her arm around his waist. "A little faith would do you a lot of good."

They sat in the library surrounded by books. The wind howled outside, making branches scratch against the windows. The sky darkened, and Dacia shoved her book across the table, laying her head on the smooth wood. Cody rubbed her shoulders while he continued reading.

When Samantha had finished with her classes for the day, she had joined them, searching book after book until she decided to try the internet. "There's quite a bit about killing Balor demons in games, but none of it is helpful in the real world unless you can find a magical sword."

"No magical swords. Just an amulet and a vase." Dacia picked up all the books she had gone through and set them on the cart. "I'm done."

She stood at the end of the table and stretched. Then she tapped her foot against the tan carpet until Samantha and Cody joined her. Cody slid his fingers through hers, rubbing his thumb over her hand while they walked back to the dorm.

Leaves blew across the sidewalks, and the wind bit into their skin.

When they got back, Dacia stood at the window, looking out into the darkness. She wouldn't eat, wouldn't drink, wouldn't sit down, and Cody didn't know what to do for her. This was her battle to face, but he wished there was some way to help her.

He walked over and put his hands on her shoulders, rubbing them, hoping to loosen them. "You okay? You haven't eaten, and you've barely said a word."

"Something's out there." Her finger shook when she pointed beneath the trees.

He wrapped his arms around her, pulled her body against his, and rested his chin on the top of her head. "Don't see anything."

"I'm scared." Her voice trembled. The sound made his heart clench.

"I know." He spun her around and lifted her chin so that she looked into his eyes. "It's gonna work out."

Chapter 25

The Time Has Come

"Dacia, wake up!" Samantha stood on Dacia's ladder, shaking her arm.

Dacia's eyes snapped open, and she stared at Samantha, blinking a few times before throwing her arms around her. "Thank God."

Cody watched them from Big Bird. His heart raced. Dacia's screams had woken him from a deep sleep, but Samantha had gotten there faster.

Dacia let go and wiped away her tears. "I thought you were dead, Samantha."

"Not dead—" she yawned "—just trying to sleep. Are you okay?"

"I'm fine." Dacia grabbed Samantha's hand. "But if I leave in the middle of the night, don't follow me."

"Why?"

She plopped back against her pillow. "Because I don't want you to die."

Cody left early in the morning, hoping to sneak through the halls before anybody was up and about. It was still dark when he hustled across the parking lot to his dorm. He looked up, hoping to see some stars, but there weren't any. The wind whipped through the trees, making branches creak and groan. Leaves fell and were tossed up again before touching the ground.

He opened the door and ran up the stairs, going into his room as silently as possible. He grabbed a change of clothes and his shower caddy and left the room without waking Drew. He hurried through his shower, not bothering to shave. As fitfully as Dacia had slept, he wanted to be there for her when she woke up.

Not wanting to walk in on Dacia or Samantha without giving them a warning first, he rapped his knuckles against the door while glancing over his shoulder. Then he stuck his key in the lock and slipped in before anybody noticed him.

Dacia sat in the corner with her knees pulled up to her chest. Her eyes were closed, and she had her hands pressed over her ears.

"Dacia." Cody raced toward her. What had happened? He looked around the room, searching for clues, but he saw nothing to explain this.

He knelt next to her. When she didn't move, he wrapped his arms around her. She hit him over and over again pummeling him with her fists until he grabbed her wrists, whispering, "Dacia, it's me. You're okay."

She opened her eyes and stared at him, but he didn't think he was what she was seeing. Her pupils were dilated, and the whites of her eyes showed all around them.

"Breathe, Dacia." He forced his voice to sound calm. "Breathe." He repeated the words over and over.

Her breathing evened out, and Cody let go of her wrists. He lifted his hand to her cheek. "Better?"

She pointed at Samantha's loft and put a finger over her lips. Then she stood up on shaking legs. Cody held onto her until she steadied. She grabbed her coat off the hook by the door and struggled to put her arms through the sleeves. Cody took it from her, holding it while she slid it on. She pulled it tighter.

They stepped into the hall, and Cody stopped in front of her, turning, looking into her eyes while he waited for her to answer.

She shook her head and shrugged.

What could have happened? Cody wondered. He'd only been gone for thirty minutes tops. He draped his arm over her shoulders and drew her against him. They walked outside.

Dacia pulled her coat even tighter, shivering the whole time, but Cody didn't think it had anything to do with the cold.

"What happened?" he finally asked.

Crimson crept up her neck and onto her face. She lowered her eyes. "Panic attack."

He thought there was more to it, but he didn't want to push her.

Cody rubbed his hand down her arm as he led her to Sedum Hall. "What do you want to do after your lesson?"

"I should read the journal or look through more books." She snuggled against him, sliding her arm inside his coat. "I'm running out of time, and I don't know how to win."

He held the door open for her. "Maybe it won't snow."

"Maybe." She shoved her hand into her pocket.

After breakfast, Dacia sat next to Cody on the couch in Sarah's office. He held her hand, but she seemed miles away. She stared out the window, and Sarah had to repeat everything that she said to her.

When they left, Dacia clutched Cody's hand. The bones in his fingers ground together, but instead of pulling them from her grip, he stopped walking and waved his hand in front of her face. "Dacia, you're out of it. Are you okay?"

"Yeah … no … I guess." She let go of his hand and raked her fingers through her hair.

"If I'm supposed to choose, I choose no." Cody tucked a strand of hair behind her ear. "You don't seem okay. I can't help you if you don't tell me what's going on."

She opened her mouth but said nothing.

His chest constricted, and his shoulders dropped. She used to tell him everything. "You don't have to … but, I want to help." He slid his hands to her shoulders. "Please let me in."

"Last night's dream is freaking me out." She gripped his arms, clutching them like she had his hand earlier. "Nefarious killed Samantha and told me he was going after you and Sarah before coming for me. I can't do this. I can't lose you guys!" Her bottom lip quivered, and tears streamed down her face. She buried her head in his chest.

Cody's heart clenched, and he wrapped his arms around her trembling body. He bent over with his mouth right next to her ear, whispering, "It's going to be okay. Everything's going to be all right. Dacia, I love you."

She nestled against him for several minutes before stepping back and pulling her gloves off. She lifted her hands to his neck. "I need to take some of your strength … not too much. Can I?"

Relieved that he could actually do something to help her, he pressed his hands down on hers. "Take it. Take it all."

She pulled his head down, then pressed her lips to his. She moved her mouth slowly at first, then pulled him closer and deepened the kiss.

Heat flared through Cody. He slid his hands under her coat, splaying them over her back.

The wind whipped around them, and Cody pulled back, yawning. He wrapped his arm around her shoulders, and they strolled to the dorm room.

Cody held the door open for Dacia. "Hello," he said to Samantha. "How you doing?"

"All right, I guess." Her voice shook.

Dacia hung her coat up. "I'm sorry about last night."

"It's not your fault." Samantha leaned forward, brushing her hair, then flipping it back and pulling it into a ponytail.

Dacia grabbed the journal and a blanket then sat down in Cookie Monster.

"Why are you looking at that again?" Samantha asked. "You've gone through it a hundred times."

"Well, maybe it's gonna take a hundred and one." Dacia snapped, then closed her eyes and rubbed the bridge of her nose. "I have to find some way to beat Nefarious, and I don't have any other ideas."

Samantha's smile was apologetic. "I don't think you're going to find any answers in there."

"Then what do you suggest?" Dacia set the journal down and leaned forward, clutching her head. "I'm out of time and out of hope."

Cody stood behind her and rubbed her shoulders. "Why're you so sure it's this weekend?"

"Before Nefarious killed Sarah, I had an ominous feeling." She stared down at her feet or the carpet or at something that only she could see there.

Samantha sat in Big Bird and leaned forward with her elbows on his knees. "Yeah?"

"I have it again now." She didn't look at either of them, just stared at that same spot. "With every passing moment, I'm more convinced something's going to happen in the next couple of days."

"Let's hope you're wrong." Cody yawned.

"Cody."

He jolted awake. Dacia knelt on the ground with her hands on his legs. "What?"

"I—" she looked up at the ceiling "—I want to go outside. It's all I can think about. I don't know if I can keep fighting it."

He reached for her, knowing that he couldn't keep her here if she wanted to go. She climbed onto his lap, curling into his arms like a child. He brushed her hair back and gently rocked the chair.

"Dacia, I want you to take my strength … all you can." His voice was sure and steady. "Take it all."

She shook her head against his chest. He could feel the action more than see it. "I can't."

"You have to." Cody traced his hand down her arm. It was the one thing he could do for her. Fighting Nefarious was in-evitable, but maybe giving her his strength would give her a chance. "If tonight's the night, take whatever you can so you can make it back to me."

"What if I hurt you … take too much?"

He lifted her hand to his lips and pressed a kiss to her knuckles. "You won't."

She slid her hands under his shirt, and he gasped, jolting into an upright position. Her fingers were freezing. She flat-tened her palms over his back and stomach. Once the initial shock wore off, he settled back, pulling her closer.

She looked up at him. "You're sure?"

"Please." The husky voice that he answered with surprised him.

She nodded and laid her head against his chest. He felt a tug beneath Dacia's hands as his energy was drawn from him and into her. It was a strange sensation, like there was a rope tied to something inside of him, and she was pulling on it. He leaned his head against the back of the chair, and his eyelids drooped. Dacia yanked her hand off his belly and tried to wiggle the other one free.

"No, Dacia." He grabbed hold of her wrist and pressed her palm against his cheek. "You need it more than me."

She drew on his energy until he fell asleep.

Cody woke up to Sarah and Samantha standing above him. He felt like he'd been sick. His strength was completely drained from him. His muscles ached. His eyes were heavy.

And Dacia was gone.

For the rest of the story, read Dacia Wolf and the Prophecy.
https://www.amazon.com/dp/1733290419

The End

The best thing that you can do to support an author,
especially an indie author, is to leave a review.

Not only do your reviews help new readers find us,
they help the algorithms guide more people to our books.
In turn, that makes it possible for us to keep writing.

Positive reviews bring a bright spot to our day,
and reviews with constructive criticism help
us figure out how to make our books better.

Acknowledgments

Writing the acknowledgments section of the book is almost as hard as writing the blurb. I don't know where to begin. What if I forget somebody? So, I would like to say: Thank you to everyone who supported my career as an author. Thank you for standing by me, lifting me up when I feel down, and for answering questions about which sounds better. If you aren't listed separately, my gratitude isn't any less.

As always, I want to thank Jeff for always being there, day in and day out for the last 33 years. Holy cow! I don't really remember life before you. (Was there life before you?)

My kiddles, Jami and Jesse, you've grown into exceptional adults, and I am so proud of you. Thank you for being so easy to raise, for being good kids, and for encouraging me.

A special thanks to three amazing authors, M.H. Woodscourt for Beta reading this book and pointing out things I missed, and Alexis D. Johnson and Caleb (C.T.) Ortega for being so supportive. It means so much to me.

If I lived a thousand years, I would never be able to repay my parents for everything they've done for me. I am so grateful God chose you for me.

Thank you!

If you liked this story, you can join my mailing list.
Drop by my website <u>MandiOyster.com</u>
or if you have any comments,
shoot me a note at mandi@mandioyster.com.
I am always happy to hear from people who've read my work.
I try to answer every email I receive.

If you liked the story, please write a short review for me.
I greatly appreciate any kind words, even one or two
sentences go a long way. The number of reviews a
book receives improves how well a book does.

Facebook: <u>https://www.facebook.com/MandiOysterAuthor</u>
Instagram: <u>https://www.instagram.com/mandioyster/</u>
My web page: MandiOyster.com

About the Author

Mandi Oyster lives in Southwest Iowa in the middle of an enchanted forest where unicorns, fairies, and dragons abound. At least, that's what she assumes when she looks out into the trees. Her husband, two kids (when they're not away at college), four cats, and two chinchillas share the house with her.

Besides being an author, she also runs her own editing business and works full-time as a digital prepress technician for a local printshop.

You can find her online at:
https://www.MandiOyster.com
https://www.facebook.com/MandiOysterAuthor
https://instagram.com/MandiOyster/

The Story Continues in ...

Dacia Wolf

AND THE PROPHECY

Book 1